MADDIE'S RECIPE OF MYSTERIES

A Rockcrest Cove Mystery Series

Book 1

Emily Page

ISBN-10: 0692564934
ISBN-13: 978-0692564936

TABLE OF CONTENTS

CHAPTER ONE

Madeline's shoes pounded out a fast staccato rhythm as she made her way down the cobblestone street to her bakery shop. She wasn't in any particular hurry, there was nothing waiting for her when she got there, nor did she have some urgent matter that needed attending to. While most people looked on and felt a bit anxious as she made her way past the tidy little row of quaint shops and peddlers on Maple Street, she was really just being her normal self.

Despite her passing the half-century mark in age, she had never really learned how to slow down and take life easy. She was just a busy woman with a lot of busy things that needed to get done. While she was finishing up one thing, her mind was already on to the next thing. So, while most people strolled down the street as they went about their business, Madeline took life at a pretty fast clip.

She wore her usual fare as she made her way to work, a pair of khakis and a simple blouse that was just long enough to cover her ample derrière, of which she had always been a bit self-conscious. And on her feet, she wore a sassy little pair of booties, shoes that resembled a boot but with the shaft cut off. The heels were at least three inches high so that she could give her five-foot, two-inch body a little more height, something else she was always self-conscious about. She knew she couldn't walk around the bakery in them all day, but at least she'd look cute walking down the street. She would change into something more sensible as soon as she got to work.

On her arm swung a large canvas bag that looked far too big for her tiny frame. The black fabric tote had a zippered top that was only half closed. If you looked closely, you'd see a white ball of fur occasionally stick its head out of the bag and look around before ducking back down into its hiding place. Her Persian cat, Astoria, was Madeline's constant companion and was with her for nearly everything she did. Quite comfortable in her homemade tote, Astoria merely wanted to know what was going on at all times. The two were inseparable even in the bakery, where Astoria spent most of her time secluded away in the back office.

At four in the morning, the streets were still quiet. The small town of Rockcrest Cove, had not awakened just yet, but in an hour or so, customers would be clamoring at her door for their morning cup of Joe and a little sweetness to go along with it. It was her practice to open up by five so that customers would not have to wait for their morning boost. Her mind was already on what she needed to do, but she knew that she had plenty of time.

Madeline rounded the corner and crossed the street and headed straight to the shop. She noticed a few lights on in other storefronts along the street but nothing was open yet. Her shop was usually the first one to open and the first to close. It was as if all the other shopkeepers followed her suit. She opened at five, the butcher across the street opened at six, the five and dime would usually open at seven, and Joe the barber next door was usually last when he opened at eight. By nine the street would be abuzz with activity, but for now, Rockcrest Cove was still asleep.

She put her key into the lock and opened the door with more force than she intended. The bells that hung on the front let out a soft tinkling sound as they experienced their first movements of the day. The smell of the sugar, butter, and coffee still lingered in the air from the day before. Madeline took in a deep breath and relished in it for just a minute.

As was her usual habit, she headed straight for the back office where she would set Astoria up for the day and change into her working shoes. But as she crossed the hallway from the kitchen to the office, a glimmer of light caught her eye. She stopped and backpedaled a few steps to get a better look. Her eyes opened wide as she confirmed her initial assumption. The back door was ajar. She quickly looked around the room and made an instant assessment of her surroundings. Nothing seemed out of place. That meant that someone had broken in or was trying to break in.

Slowly she put her bag down and looked around for a weapon. Her heart beating a little faster, she took careful, deliberate steps as she reached for the nearest thing she could find: a baker's rolling pin. She tested its heft by holding one end to make sure that it would do the trick if she needed to use it. Satisfied, she brandished it over her right shoulder, holding it in place with both hands, and she stealthily crept toward the door.

With each step she became more frustrated that she had not changed her noisy booties she had worn to work. The steel toe and heel made what seemed to be an awful clicking sound with every move. She finally decided to shed them about halfway down the hall. As she approached the door in her bare socks, she gingerly pushed it open with one hand and stood back with her rolling pin ready just in case someone charged, but the door swung back silently with no particular fanfare.

She pushed again, and again nothing happened. The third time she held the door open and peeped out into the alley. In the darkness, it was difficult to make out anything clearly. It took a moment for her eyes to adjust before she was able to see a solitary figure lying near the dumpsters.

Just a homeless person, she thought, and her confidence returned. Dropping her pin, she now felt a little indignant about the intrusion on her property. She stepped out the door and approached the figure, ready to let them have it with a good piece of her mind, but stopped short just a few feet away. The body wasn't moving; there was something eerie and strange about the way it was laying there. Even in the darkness she could see that something was wrong.

The body appeared twisted and contorted in a way that told her that life had already left this person behind. The skin had that odd grayish hue, and the eyes were vacant pools that used to be brown. The hands were twisted in such a way to show that she had been struggling and grasping for each breath, as she knew her life was ebbing away from her.

Madeline suddenly went from investigative mode to recognition. Slowly the realization dawned on her that she knew this person. A shudder ran through her as her old rival's lifeless body lay there just outside her door.

Without realizing it, her body made an involuntary scream that seemed to be far more powerful than her tiny body should have been able to produce. For a moment she stood absolutely frozen in place as the reality of the sight settled in her mind. Within seconds, Joe, the barber next door, was running in her direction, but Madeline had yet to move.

In the darkness, he almost ran right up on the body before he realized what was before him. He stopped short, surveying the horrific scene in front of him. For a moment he seemed to be in a quandary as to what to do; should he help Madeline, who clearly seemed distraught and nearly at the point of hysteria, or should he phone the police and get them the help they needed?

"Maddie," he asked. "Are you ok?"

Madeline didn't answer. She stood stock still, frozen in place as if her feet were rooted to the ground underneath her.

"Maddie." He spoke again, but still there was no response.

Joe reached into his pocket for his cell phone but remembered that he had left it inside his shop.

"Maddie," he said, "I'll be right back."

He held his hand out in front of him as if he was going to touch her, but he never made contact.

"I'm going to go and get some help."

He turned and ran back to his store as fast as he could, his feet making a soft pounding sound, breaking the silence of the early morning.

Madeline remained rooted to her spot as though she was a statue welded in place. Slowly the shock of the sight began to wear off, and Madeline realized that her relationship was over. A new feeling began to emerge, one of sadness and disappointment. She tentatively took a step towards Emma's body and spoke softly to her, as if she could still hear her voice.

"Oh, Emma," she started. "I'm so sorry about everything." She cried.

The body still lay there unmoving, but Madeline began speaking as though it were some type of cathartic release.

"I didn't mean to hurt you," she continued.

"I – I wish that I had been able to see the talent you had when I first hired you, but it was my own desire for the limelight that made me block out everything but what I wanted."

She paused for just a minute as the flood of emotions began to take its toll. Her body trembled from the shock that was settling in.

"I'm sorry that I beat you in all those competitions we fought over," she mumbled in a low undertone.

It felt good, and it seemed to ease her shock a bit to be able to speak so openly and honestly with her rival lying at her feet.

"I should have let you take the lead in the kitchen like you wanted, you had some ideas for new recipes and I never listened to you."

A sudden noise at the other end of the alley brought her up short. She looked in the way of Joe's shop to see if he was coming back but saw nothing. She heard the noise again and looked down the narrow thoroughfare and noticed a darkened figure at the other end. Horror and fear fleeted across her face as she realized she was not alone. Was the killer still there? What did he hear? Had someone been watching her the whole time?

CHAPTER TWO

By the time the first glimmer of light began to reach the town, activity around Madeline's bakery was in full swing. If the sight of yellow tape across the entrance of the building was not enough to deter the customers from their early morning rituals, certainly the sight of a uniformed police officer standing guard was enough to do the trick. Still, while they knew that they couldn't enter the store and start their day as they usually did, there was little motivation for them to go on about their daily business.

Rockcrest Cove was a small town, and this was probably the most excitement they'd seen in years.

Many stood nearby with their phones at the ready, prepared to capture any moment they could on camera so they could discuss and debate with family and friends for days, weeks, and maybe even months or years.

Rita and Sandra, her two employees, had arrived shortly after the police and were immediately shuttled into the back office. The two girls were visibly stunned but were able to maintain their composure nevertheless. Madeline sat in her office chair, still with a dazed look on her face, but she had been able to regain some level of her original composure. The immediate shock of her discovery was beginning to wear off, and the reality of the events now unfolding before her eyes was becoming painfully clear.

Chief Edward Nolan was standing in the back doorway where Madeline had first discovered the body. His eyes were surveying the scene but his body language told a different story. He looked irritated that this crime had interfered with his sleep.

"Martin!" he shouted.

"Yes, Chief." Deputy Martin was immediately at his side.

"What've you got?"

"Not much, sir," he started.

He reached into his back pocket and pulled out a regulation police notebook and began to read off his notes.

"The victim's name is Emma Larson, a former employee and coworker of Mrs. McDougal. It appears that a single gunshot wound to the chest was the cause of death, but that will have to be confirmed by the coroner."

"Who found the body?" he asked gruffly.

"Mrs. McDougal, sir."

Nolan went into a deep thought process for a minute.

"Larson, Larson," he said more to himself than to the deputy by his side.

"Why does that name sound familiar?" he said, thinking out loud.

Rockcrest Cove was a pretty small town and everyone knew everyone else. He paced the floor of the narrow hallway for a minute while he racked his brain trying to figure out where he knew that name. He stopped suddenly. Carefully placing his index finger on the tip of his nose, he started thinking out loud.

"Wasn't she another baker here in town?"

The chief's left eyebrow shot up as he made the connection. A little half smile passed over his lips.

"Well, well, well. I may be able to go home and finish my rest after all." The town was small enough that rivalries were never a secret.

"What's that, sir?"

"Mrs. McDougal found the body, the deceased was a former employee of hers, and they were both in a long-time rivalry. It seems pretty obvious what happened here."

"But, sir," Martin interjected, "shouldn't we get a forensic team in here before we draw any conclusions?"

"Listen here, deputy. I've been doing this a long time. I've been solving cases like this since long before we got a forensic team here. Where is Mrs. McDougal?" he demanded. "I can solve this case right now."

"Um, she's in the office, sir."

Martin pointed toward the office door and turned and left the room before any more of an exchange could occur.

Nolan entered the office and surveyed the room. The three women sat silently in their prospective corners, each lost in their own thoughts. He felt a little proud of himself, satisfied that he had already solved the case. The only thing left for him to do was to get a signed confession. In his mind, he could already see the mayor bestowing him with honors for his swift action.

He pulled up a chair across from Madeline. "Mrs. McDougal," he started.

"Do you want to tell me what happened?" he asked.

"Everyone calls me Maddie," she said, her voice stoic and numb.

"What?" He paused for just a beat as he processed her statement. "Oh, yes. Ok. So, Madeline, can you tell me what happened?"

Madeline sat with her hands on her desk, nervously fingering the rim of the cup of coffee she was supposed to be drinking.

"Well, like I told the other officer, I was just getting to work this morning and I noticed that the back door was ajar. So I decided to go and investigate."

Nolan eyes surveyed his suspect's tiny frame. "You. Investigate."

"Yes."

"With what?" he asked, almost as if to mock her. She didn't look like she was strong enough to take on any burglar.

"A rolling pin." She chuckled a bit to herself as she thought about confronting a criminal with a rolling pin. "I guess I wasn't thinking right."

"I suppose not."

"Anyway, when I opened the door that's when I saw the body."

Her voice trailed off as the vision of Emma's body lying on the cold hard ground of the back alley filled her mind.

"Who was with you?" Nolan prodded.

"It was only me. I usually open up first and then the girls come in a little later.

"So, you were here alone when the murder happened."

"I-I-I don't know when the murder happened. I was here alone when I found her," Madeline corrected.

"How convenient," Nolan scoffed.

The pupils of Madeline's eyes slowly begin to dilate as she caught Nolan's tone.

"Wha!" She exclaimed. "You can't possibly mean that I…No, I couldn't…"

She was unable to finish her statement. The shock of it all was overwhelming at best.

Chief Nolan removed his square-rimmed glasses and looked directly into her eyes.

"Well what do you expect me to believe?"

He began counting off his assumptions on his fingers.

"You discovered the body, she was your employee, and you were long-time rivals."

It took only a minute before Madeline's mind registered the sideways accusation. She sat there staring at the chief, her mouth agape as she processed the situation.

"Aren't you going to investigate?"

Nolan rose from his seat and looked around the room.

"Not much need for that when you have the number one suspect right in front of you, is there?"

Chief Nolan turned away from Madeline and started slowly toward the door.

She was speechless for just a heartbeat while the weight of the accusation hung over her head.

"But, you are going to investigate, aren't you?" she asked again to confirm.

Nolan turned at the door to face her.

"I already have," he said a little too cockily for her taste.

"Don't go anywhere," he added. "I'll be right back."

He turned and walked out the door without ever looking back.

Appalled, Madeline looked across the room at Rita and Sandra, both of who had a look of shock and dismay on their faces. They had heard the entire exchange. The shock of earlier events was now eclipsed by this horrific accusation. Madeline sat in stony silence for a minute before Rita spoke up.

"Ms. Maddie," she said, "you have to call someone."

Madeline said nothing in response; she was trying to compose herself. The stress was beginning to get the best of her.

"Ms. Madeline." Rita inserted her voice more forcefully to interrupt her thoughts.

This time Madeline's eyes slowly turned in her direction. The fire burning in them was plain to see.

"Call Bailey," Rita said softly. "Call her now. Before they come back."

She pointed her head toward the door.

Madeline nodded in agreement and fumbled in her bag for her cell phone. She quickly hit the button that said Bailey and waited for the phone to ring.

Bailey was still sleeping when the phone jolted her out of a pleasant dream. She let out a groan as the shrill sound pierced her sleep cycle, ripping her from her precious sleep. She opened her eyes just a crack as she looked at the clock. 4:50! Who in their right mind would be calling at 4:50 in the morning? Her initial thought was to disconnect and let it ring through, but then that sudden rush of fear ran through her. Phones don't usually ring that early in the morning unless someone has died or has been in an accident. Quickly she rolled over and checked her caller ID. It was her gran.

Strange, she thought. She should be at the bakery at this hour. Something must be wrong. She snatched up the phone and answered.

"Hello."

Bailey's voice had that raspy sound that said that she had just woken up.

"Hello, Bailey."

"Good morning, Gran," Bailey responded. She could instantly tell that something was not right.

"What's wrong?"

Madeline had a difficult time getting the words to come to her mouth.

"Something terrible has happened," she finally managed to say.

"What?"

Bailey asked again, her heart pounding a little too rapidly for that hour of the morning.

"Emma Larson is dead,"

Madeline forced herself to say.

"She was found outside the store this morning, and the police think I did it."

She blurted out the rest of the information all at once. There. It was all out there now. She wouldn't have to speak the horrible details about it anymore.

"What!?" Bailey was suddenly fully alert. "Don't be absurd!" she exclaimed, her anger rising. "Where are you?"

"I'm at the store right now."

Nolan came back into the office and Madeline had to lower her voice into the phone. She gave a sideways glance at Nolan, who was watching her suspiciously from the doorway.

"Who are you talking to?" he asked.

"M-m-my granddaughter," Madeline managed to say.

Bailey spoke into the phone, saying, and "Is that him?"

"Yes," Madeline said quietly.

"What's his name?" she asked.

Madeline didn't want to speak while Chief Nolan was still in the room. For some reason she didn't want him to know she was talking about him, probably an old self-conscious habit from her school days. So, she just held the phone and said nothing.

It was Nolan who broke the silence instead.

"Why don't you hang up the phone right now, and we'll talk some more."

Madeline was now beginning to lose her patience. She stared at Nolan with eyes that cut through him like daggers.

"I am talking to my granddaughter, and unless you are charging me with a crime, I see no reason why I can't speak with her."

Nolan, a man who was not accustomed to being disrespected so openly, looked around the room to make sure that none of his deputies had overheard her. Satisfied that he was the only officer in the room, he lowered his voice.

"Mrs. McDougal, I am trying to be nice to you, but if you insist on this attitude, maybe we should continue our conversation down at the station."

Madeline looked incredulous. "Are you arresting me?"

The tiny sound of Bailey's voice came from the phone. A barely audible

"He can't do that!" was heard through the line.

Madeline turned her attention back to the phone and listened carefully as Bailey gave her instructions.

Now wide awake, Bailey hung up the phone, her anger rising with every breath. She sat on the edge of her bed and thought for a minute. She had to help her gran. After only a minute, she snatched up the phone and started to dial a number. She hesitated for just a second and looked at her clock. It was only a little after five in the morning, maybe it was too early to call.

Oh to hell with it, she thought to herself, and finished dialing the number.

The police station was a dark and dingy place that looked like it hadn't been updated at all in the past hundred years. That dark wood paneling made the place look gloomy and depressing in comparison to the rest of town. Rockcrest Cove was small, but it had a quiet energy that spoke of small town values but with a large spirit. Everyone knew each other and took care of each other.

Already the news of the murder was spreading like a forest fire out of control. The wagging tongues were going to be hard for Madeline to overcome, but in time, this news would fade and someone else's misfortune would take its place. That was the nature of life in a town like Rockcrest Cove.

So, when Bailey and Kyle walked into the police station an hour later, it was obvious that the news had already begun to spread, even at this ungodly hour. Immediately upon entering, Bailey could see a few people in the waiting room lean into each other, raise their hands surreptitiously as if to hide the sight of their lips moving. Subconsciously she wondered why they bothered; it was obvious that they were talking about her gran. A few women cut cat eyes at Bailey and Kyle as they walked past them and up to the front desk.

Kyle was a tall and lean fellow, but already you could tell that his life as a lawyer was treating him well. One could already see that he was doing well as a lawyer and the good life was beginning to make changes even in his physical appearance. So far he was still able to maintain that fine, muscular physique that he was once so proud of. Now, however, his work was done behind a desk and he found less time to work out like he used to. As a new lawyer, he was eager to take on a new case, so when Bailey called him that morning, he had no problem letting go of his pillow and getting moving. He was just waiting for the right client, and Madeline McDougal was exactly what he needed to give his new burgeoning practice a boost.

After talking to the desk sergeant, they headed down a long corridor toward a bank of rooms at the far end. They entered the room without knocking. Madeline was sitting in a small room with bare walls and a solitary table in the center. A picture immediately emerged and took shape in Bailey's mind, and she had a hard time keeping silent, as Kyle had instructed her to do. Nolan's large frame was frozen in place as he stood there towering over Madeline with his fists planted on the desk, looking like large tree trunks rooted to its surface, refusing to budge even in the fiercest of winds; his deputy was standing farther back by the door, a silent observer.

Kyle quickly surveyed the scene and then spoke.

"Chief Nolan, can I have a word with you?"

Nolan's face turned beet red as he tried to keep his anger in check.

"I'm interviewing a suspect. "Nolan said. "Do you mind?"

"Actually, I do mind," Kyle replied.

"This is my client, and I've not had the chance to consult with her yet."

Nolan opened his mouth to say something, but Kyle deftly held his hand up and stopped him before he could speak.

"Before you launch your objections, Chief, I'd like to ask a few questions of my own."

Kyle positioned himself between Madeline and Nolan.

"Is my client under arrest?"

Nolan hesitated for just a second before he responded.

"No, she's not under arrest, but she's certainly a person of interest."

"I see," Kyle said.

His voice had that measured quality that only attorneys knew how to deliver.

"And did you offer her legal representation before you brought her in for questioning?"

Nolan looked dumbfounded. He stared at the young man with a clear look of disdain.

"Are you trying to tell me how to do my job?"

He fell back on his usual argument when someone new to law would question him.

"I have been doing this job for more than—"Kyle's hand went up again.

"Chief Nolan, I understand that you've been on your job for more than 40 years, so I'm sure I don't have to tell you that anyone considered a suspect in a crime has the right to have an attorney present before questioning. And I'm sure that you informed Mrs. McDougal of her rights before you started your proceedings."

"She's not a suspect. She's a person of interest in this case," Nolan defended.

"Oh," Kyle said, "she's not a suspect. Then she's free to go."

Without another word he turned to Bailey.

"Bailey, please take your grandmother and go. I'll meet up with you later at your house."

Bailey and Madeline took their cue and left Kyle and Chief Nolan to duke it out. Before they reached the end of the hallway, they could already hear Nolan's voice bellowing out of the darkness, clearly irate at and infuriated by being undercut by the young attorney.

CHAPTER THREE

Madeline sat quietly at Bailey's kitchen counter; her thoughts seemed to be all over the place. Her mind was searching for an answer that would explain how she had gotten to this place. Her hand caressed a cup of coffee as she pondered her predicament. She had been so happy this morning as she left for a job that she thoroughly loved, and suddenly she had been plummeted into this quandary without any explanation.

She and Emma had been on opposite sides of the same goals for years. They had attended the same schools, in fact, sometimes even the same classes. They had the same goals and dreams. Now she suddenly felt empty as she thought about the long-term rivalry they had shared over the years. Without a doubt, it was certainly a love-hate relationship. She let her mind drift back a few years as she mulled over the developments that lead up to this day.

Emma had mixed feelings as she walked through the doorway of the new bakery that was about to open. She wore a smart, grey two-piece suit that bespoke a woman that was all about business. Her sensible black shoes were certainly not a style that she felt comfortable with but for a job interview it was the best choice. She didn't see herself walking in with a nice pair of stilettos for a job at a bakery shop. As a matter of fact, she wasn't entirely sure that the suit was the best choice for the interview either.

She had debated whether or not to just put on a nice pair of designer jeans instead. After all, this wasn't going to be the standard interview. She and Madeline went way back. She felt a mild irritation that she even had to go to the interview. After all, they were about as equal as you could get. In her heart of hearts, she felt she should have been a partner in the business rather than someone looking for an entry-level job. It wasn't fair, she thought to herself, but nevertheless she had to play the part.

She stood in the middle of the storefront and looked around. The place was almost ready to open for business and she could feel that it would be a success. Madeline always had a really good sense of style, and her charming personality could already be seen in the little accents around the store: the decorative tablecloths, the pale pink stenciling on the walls, and the quaint little his and hers signs on the bathroom doors. Yes, it was oozing Madeline. Emma wanted to be just a little bit sick at the thought of it.

Madeline appeared from the back dressed in her usual khakis and long blouse. Does the woman ever wear anything different, she thought to herself, but on her face she wore a bright smile deftly hiding her inner feelings.

"Madeline," she said as she stuck out her hand in her direction.

"It's so good to see you again. How long has it been?" she asked with a smile.

"Oh, Emma." Madeline responded.

"I was so happy you called."

She gave her friend a genuine smile as she took her hand.

"Yes, yes, it has been a bit too long. I was so happy you called about the job. I honestly didn't know what I was going to do. I certainly can't handle all of this work by myself."

"Why, Maddie." Emma smiled. "You know you can always count on me for support."

"I so appreciate that. Why don't you come in the back so we can talk?"

"I'd like that," Emma answered.

Together the two women walked through the maze of the half-finished bakery toward the office.

"Have a seat." Madeline gestured toward an empty chair across from her desk.

"Thank you," Emma accepted.

Her eyes were surreptitiously surveying her surroundings. A little twinge of jealousy got the better of her for the moment, but she quickly put it in check.

"Can I get you anything? Coffee? Tea?"

"No, thank you. I didn't expect that you would have anything ready to serve already."

Madeline took a seat behind her desk and carefully surveyed the woman across from her.

"Well," she said, "everything is coming along quite nicely and we're right on schedule.

"When do you plan to open?"

"We're scheduled to open in three weeks. By then the construction will be completed and all the equipment will be in place."

Madeline chuckled a little.

"As a matter of fact, I'm a little surprised too. I never thought that it would be so easy to get a store up and running."

Madeline gazed about the room and felt a sense of pride at her accomplishments. But she quickly snapped out of her revelry and got back to business.

"Well, why don't we get started, shall we?"

"Of course," Emma agreed. "Although I think it's a little strange that you're interviewing me. I mean we were in the same class in school."

Madeline chuckled. "I guess you're right. I already know more about you than I need to know."

Emma tried hard not to roll her eyes as she smiled at Madeline across the desk. The woman was utterly clueless, she thought. She really believes that we are all her friends. Her jealousy began to rise again. She knew she should've been the one behind the desk, with the new business, and the financial backing.

"So." Madeline cut into her thoughts.

"What kind of job are you looking for?" Madeline asked.

Emma was fighting hard to maintain her composure.

"Well, how about a job as a baker?" she replied, trying hard to keep out the bitter taste the words were forming in her mouth.

"Well, we can certainly handle that," Madeline replied.

"But do you have a specialty?" she asked. "What's your favorite thing to do in the kitchen?"

I don't believe she's going to actually go through the interview process! Emma thought with amazement. She gripped her fingers a little tighter around the purse she held in her lap but still continued to smile at Madeline, but by now her lips were beginning to get a little taut from the effort.

"Ah, yeah, I do," she managed. "But you already know that, don't you?"

Madeline looked a little confused for a minute before recognizing what her old friend had been referring to. The two of them had entered a baking contest before, and they had used her specialty, a spiced coconut cake, as the entry.

"Yes, I suppose I do. It was the recipe that got me started on my career."

There was a bit of silence in the room for just a beat too long. Finally Madeline spoke.

"Well, I don't see the need to continue with this," she said.

"As you've already stated, I already know you well. After all, our years together in school should be enough to show me that you'd be a great addition to my staff." She paused for just a beat.

"Welcome aboard," she said as she offered her hand to Emma.

Gratefully, Emma accepted the hand, glad the charade was over.

"We'll start on Monday. What do you think?"

"Monday? I though you weren't opening for three weeks."

"Yes, that's correct. But we still need to order supplies, set up the kitchen, and stock the shelves. If we want to be ready on time, I could use the extra hands."

"Hands?"

"Yes, I hired two other girls as well."

The two women rose from their seats and smiled at each other and gave a hearty handshake to seal the deal.

Bailey's voice cut into Madeline's thoughts. "Gran, are you ok?"

Madeline gave her granddaughter a genuine smile.

"Yes, I'm fine. I was just thinking about Emma."

Bailey gave her gran a look of understanding.

"I'm sorry about what happened, Gran, but you know as well as I that she wasn't as sweet as the pies she made. It was just a matter of time before something happened to her."

Madeline said, "Yes, I know, dear. But no one deserves what happened to her."

Bailey was hardly sympathetic to the cause.

"Well, Kyle will be here shortly. Why don't you just rest a bit while I get some breakfast going."

"Fine, dear."

Bailey handed her a blanket and Madeline curled herself up on the sofa to try to get a little rest. Her mind began to drift again.

~~~

Emma had arrived at work the following Monday wearing more sensible clothes than she did for the interview. A crisp pair of designer jeans and a T-shirt were the obvious choice. Madeline surveyed Emma's attire and wondered if she had been clear enough when she told her what she would do. Those nice jeans were going to be ruined by the end of the day.

"Emma, are you sure that's what you want to wear? We're going to be getting really dirty today."

Emma looked down at her attire. "What's wrong with what I'm wearing?"

"It's just that we're going to be moving a lot of things around. Those are nice jeans. I'd hate for something to happen to them."

"Well, I guess I've been duly warned," she quipped, and walked on toward the back of the store.

Madeline stared after her for a moment. Well, she thought, Emma always did have a mind of her own.

Rita and Sandra were already in the back sorting out newly delivered supplies and trying to decide how to organize everything.

Madeline followed Emma into the room.

"Let me introduce you all. Emma, this is Rita and this is Sandra. They'll be working with us here at the bakery."

Emma gave them a smile. "Oh, really. Where did you study?"

Both girls gave her an odd look. Rita spoke first.

"Well, I went to Scottsdale High."

"Me too," Sandra chimed in.

Emma was speechless for just a moment.

"High school?" she questioned.

She gave Madeline a sideways glance. She couldn't be serious. These girls weren't even out of diapers yet, and Madeline has her working with them. She was appalled.

"Well, nice to meet you," she said.

Madeline broke the silence.

"Why don't you two get started in the kitchen while Emma and I work on setting up the office?"

"Sure, Mrs. McDougal."

"Let's not stand on formality. I don't much like being called Mrs. McDougal. Why don't you call me Maddie?" she suggested.

The young girls smiled and nodded as they left the room. As soon as they were clear, Emma rounded on Maddie.

"Are you serious? High school kids?"

"Well, their jobs don't require that much detail. They'll learn as they go. Think of them as your interns."

Madeline tried to lighten the already tense moment. Already she was beginning to regret what she had begun to realize was maybe a mistake.

"Yeah, well, they better stay out of my way,"

Emma quipped before settling down to work. But her ire was up and she had to get something off her chest.

"You know, you're the one that should really be working for me," she said with a light smile.

"After all, I've been in the kitchen just as long as you have."

"Perhaps," Maddie agreed. "But why didn't you open your own shop when you had the chance?"

"You know as well as I do that I didn't have the money, and I couldn't get a loan."

"Oh, yeah, that's right," She said. "I forgot."

"If I'd had the money, I would've been able to beat you at that competition."

Maddie understood what she was referring to. The annual Baker's Competition sponsored by their alma mater had been the turning point in her life. Her winning first place in the competition got her the recognition she needed to get the backing for her new store. Had she not won the competition, the conversation she and Emma were having at that moment would have been very different.

"Well, thank you for coming in second place." Maddie smiled. "You changed my life."

"I know," Emma replied. "I should've been the one to win. After all, the recipe was my idea."

Maddie recoiled for just a second.

"If I recall, we all developed the recipe together, but you and Evan decided to pull out at the last minute and reenter as singles." Maddie thought for minute.

"As I remember, I found the final ingredients that gave the cupcakes the unique flavor that won the competition. Had you stayed with us, we could've all shared in the glory."

Emma's eyes rolled back in her head, but Madeline didn't see it.

"Well, I swore that day that I would beat you at the next baking competition."

Maddie turned away from her desk where she had been organizing bills.

"Why didn't you?" She asked. "I mean, I know you were good. Why didn't you enter the competition the next year?"

Emma's face turned red and she didn't answer. She didn't want to give Maddie the satisfaction of knowing that she had been sleeping with one of the professors at school and didn't want the news to come out.

"Well, there's another competition coming up in three months. Why don't you enter then?"

"Maybe I will," Emma finally replied.

"Maybe I will," she said a little more slowly, as an idea was beginning to form in her head.

"By the way, whatever happened to Evan? Weren't the two of you pretty close?"

"Yes, we were,"

Emma answered, thankful for the change of subject.

"And his sister, Rachel. He does private catering. You know, weddings, private parties, and stuff like that. He's doing quite well."

"And his sister?"

"Well, you know. Rachel is Rachel."

"Yes, I do," Maddie said.

She had never really liked Rachel. Wherever the girl went, it seemed like trouble would inevitably follow. There was never really anything specific she could put her finger on, but she knew that something was not good about the trio. She was glad they were no longer together. Maybe Emma would rise to her potential without that negative influence.

The doorbell rang and Maddie was back in the present. She saw Bailey fly from the kitchen to the living room to answer the door. She looked just a little too eager to get to Kyle. I wonder what's going on with those two, Madeline thought, but that was all the time she had to debate the possibilities. She had more pressing matters to attend to at the moment. She got up from her relaxing position on the sofa and went in to greet her new, young attorney.

CHAPTER FOUR

Once again Madeline found herself back at the dreary looking police station. This time it was her choice. Kyle had encouraged her to go in and make an official statement about what had happened the morning she discovered Emma's body. She was relieved when she arrived and discovered that Nolan had not yet come in. She wanted to get through the statement and be gone before he arrived, but luck was not on her side that day.

With Kyle on one side and Bailey on the other, she sat at the dinky little table with a microphone in front of her. Deputy Martin, who had been at the store on that morning just three days ago, was asking the questions. Things were going quite well and she felt relaxed and a little more herself until the door flung open with a loud, banging noise as it slammed against the wall. Nolan's mighty bulk entered the room and seemed to suck all of the oxygen out of it.

"What's going on here?" he demanded.

"We're just taking Mrs. McDougal's statement, sir," Martin replied.

"We don't need a damn statement," he said. "We need a confession."

"Why would I confess to something I didn't do?" Maddie protested.

Nolan gave her a look of derision. He'd had a chance to mull over the case in the few days since he'd seen her and was more convinced than ever that Madeline had committed the crime. He only needed to prove it.

"Sir," Martin added, "this is standard procedure when investigating any case. We have to get a statement from everyone involved."

"She's more than involved," Nolan commented.

Kyle got up from his seat. "If that's the case, chief," he started, "then why are you so opposed to her making a statement?"

"It's a waste of taxpayer dollars," Nolan complained.

Not that he particularly cared about the taxpayers. He just didn't have anything else to say that would justify his argument.

"Well, chief," Kyle continued,

"if you insist on denying my client's rights, if and when you do find any evidence, you won't be able to build up a case against her. But all of that is really moot, since my client is innocent."

"How can you say she's innocent?" Nolan shouted.

"She was the only one at the scene, they had a life-long rivalry, and she was seen by witnesses standing over the body."

"Standing over the body, at her place of business where she has worked for years. Chief, you don't have any evidence to charge her."

"But I will," Nolan stated. "Just give me time."

"May I ask"—Kyle spoke again—"are you pursuing any other possible suspects?"

"Why should I?" Nolan said defiantly.

"That's all I need to know," Kyle said as he reached his hand in his pocket and pulled out a small recorder. He held up the recorder to the Chief.

"That's all I need to know."

He turned to Bailey and Madeline. "This procedure is over. Ladies," He said and opened the door for them.

The two ladies silently stood up and walked out of the room with Kyle following them.

Outside, the three of them met on the steps of the police station.

"The man is an incompetent boob," Maddie complained, clearly irritated by the stubbornness of the old chief.

"That he is,"

Kyle agreed as he steered the women in the direction he wanted them to go.

"It doesn't sound like he's going to even try to find the real killer," Bailey whined. "What are we going to do?"

Maddie had had just about as much as she could take. "I know what I'm going to do," she said.

"I can do a better job of investigating a murder than that idiot."

"Gran, what are you saying?" Bailey asked, concerned.

"I'm saying that if I don't want to be the one and only suspect in this case, I have to deliver them another suspect. I have to investigate the case myself."

A bit of her spirit was finally returning, and both Bailey and Kyle could see that the old Maddie was back.

Kyle looked a little concerned. "I'm not sure it'll be safe for you to get into this yourself, Maddie."

"I know what you're saying, Kyle," she agreed.

"But I don't think I have a choice. That man is out to get me, and unless I do something about it, he's going to find a way to charge me for Emma's murder."

"There's no way he can charge you with the murder, Maddie. He has no case," Kyle assured her.

"Yes, but as long as he believes I'm the killer, he has no reason to look for anyone else either," she countered.

"And the real murderer gets to go free."

Kyle looked at his watch and knew he didn't have the time to debate the issue at the moment.

"Why don't we meet later to discuss it?"

"Well, the shop is cleared to reopen. But now it's empty. Why don't we meet there this afternoon?" Maddie suggested.

"Fine with me," Bailey said. "I have class soon anyway."

"All right, this afternoon. Three o'clock?" he suggested.

The three said their good-byes and went their separate ways.

Maddie was busy cleaning up the bakery when Bailey arrived. She had hardly noticed the time had gone by so quickly. The police had done a thorough investigation, but they weren't that good about cleaning up after themselves. They had gone through everything in the store and had left nothing untouched. She was beginning to worry that she wouldn't have everything back in order to reopen the next day.

When Bailey arrived a little before three, she found her gran bent over inside one of the display cases, trying to clean the glass from the inside. She chuckled a little to herself as she watched the older woman try to extricate herself from her awkward position.

"Oh, Bailey," she said. "Is it three already?"

"Almost," Bailey replied. "I'm a little early."

Maddie straightened and stretched her stiff back and mopped her brow with her forearm.

"I'm afraid the police left me with way too much work to reopen for tomorrow." She made a sweeping gesture with her arm.

"Look at this mess."

Indeed it was a mess. A line of dirty footprints that lead from the front of the store all the way to the back door was apparent. In the kitchen, things had been moved and analyzed. There was a fine dusting of flour over everything, and the equipment and tools were all out of place.

"I don't know what they did with all of these ingredients; they left the containers all open so I can't use them," Maddie complained.

"I have to toss it all and reorder fresh supplies."

Bailey gave a sad sigh for her gran. "I'll help," she said as she rolled up her sleeves. "What do you want me to do?"

Maddie gave her granddaughter a gentle smile. She could always count on her when she needed help the most.

"Well, Kyle will be here soon…"

"So you better give me something to do before he gets here. No need to waste time," she said. "Chop, chop."

Maddie grinned at the girl. "That line belongs in a Chinese restaurant, not an elite bakery."

They both laughed together and set about restoring the store back to its original glory.

They hadn't made much progress when they heard the chimes over the door. Kyle arrived in a rush of activity. He seemed much more excited than he had been earlier that morning.

"Good afternoon, ladies," he said while he busied himself by pulling up a table and a few chairs."

"Wow. You seem excited," Bailey noted.

"Indeed, I am. Come have a seat. Let me tell you what I discovered."

Kyle carefully pulled his small laptop from his briefcase and set it on the table so that both of the women could see.

"I started thinking after I left you that we need to know more about Emma in order to find out why anyone would want to kill her."

"You should've asked me," said Madeline.

"I've known her for years, and I can assure you that there are a lot of people that hated her. She was an arrogant, pushy little thing, and it was hard to stomach her sometimes."

Kyle gave Madeline an appraising look. The words that came from her did not match the Madeline that Bailey always talked about.

"Humph," was all he said at that time, but he made note in his mind to check into the relationship

Madeline and Emma had had. Apparently there was no love lost between them. Instead, he directed his attention back to his laptop.

"Well, I did some checking and I found out something." He started clicking away at his keyboard.

"Do you know anyone named Evan Foster?"

Madeline's face revealed instant recognition.

"Yes, I know Evan. He, Emma, and I all went to the same school together."

"Really," Kyle said as he continued to click through his keyboard.

"Why?" Madeline asked.

"Do you think that Evan had something to do with Emma's death?" she asked, surprised.

"Well, read this and tell me what you think."

He pushed his laptop closer to the two women even though neither of them really needed it.

Both women leaned in to see a press release about Evan Foster opening up his own bakery on the other side of town. Madeline's eyes visibly dilated as she read the article, and an obvious spark of recollection appeared across her face for a brief second.

"Oh my," she said.

"What?" Kyle asked. "Did you remember something?"

"Oh, nothing," Madeline covered.

"It's just been a long time since I've heard anything about Evan. Just brings back some old memories, is all."

Kyle eyed her cautiously but he didn't pursue it for now. He had a strong hunch that Madeline was holding back, but he wanted to be sure before he pursued it any further.

"Did you know that Evan had his own bakery across town?" Kyle asked.

"No.

The last I heard he was running a successful catering business after we all finished school.

How did this come up in connection to Emma?"

"Interestingly enough, look who it says was his partner." Kyle pointed at the line in the article.

"His partner was Emma?" Bailey asked in disbelief.

"When did this open?" Madeline asked.

She had the urge to grab the paper and rifle through it, but these modern computers took that privilege away from her.

"Two years ago," Kyle answered.

"Two years ago!" Bailey resounded. "She was still working for you?"

Madeline sat silently, thinking to herself. There was more going on than she had originally thought. Could it be? Were they that envious that they would have conspired against her that way? She resisted the urge to tell Bailey and Kyle what she was thinking until she could be absolutely sure of her doubts. She was not about to accuse anybody of such a heinous crime unless she had absolute proof.

The three of them continued to discuss the relationship that Emma and Evan had secretly held over the last few years and wondered what else about her they didn't know.

It was well into the evening before the three of them broke up and went their separate ways.

"Need a ride home, Gran?" Bailey asked.

"No, dear. I'm going to stay behind and do a little more cleaning up. I need to get my store back in order so I can reopen."

"Gran, why don't you hire a service to do that? They can come in here and have it all done in a day. It'll be worth the investment."

Madeline laughed at her granddaughter. "What are you going to be? A business lawyer?"

Bailey laughed too. "No, it's just that I don't like to see you so stressed out about things. I know how much this store means to you."

"That's why doing it myself is so therapeutic," Madeline answered.

"When I'm stressed, I come here and work things out while I'm baking. I need to do this myself. It's my stress reliever."

"All right, Gran. Just don't stay here too late."

"I won't. Astoria and I will be home before you know it."

"I have classes tomorrow, but I can come and give you a hand afterward."

"I'd like that," Madeline agreed. "Now go on home, I have a lot of work to do."

"Make sure you lock the door behind me."

"I will." The two walked to the door, arms around each other. Bailey gave her gran a long hard look.

"Are you sure you're ok?"

She asked as she lovingly pushed a stray strand of hair away from her face.

"I'm fine," Madeline assured her. "Don't worry about me. I'll see you tomorrow."

She watched as Bailey left the building and walked across the street to where her car was parked. As soon as everyone left, Astoria came out of her usual hiding place and rubbed up against Maddie's leg. She picked her up and gave her a gentle hug.

"Ah, Astoria," She said as she looked the cat in the face.

"You and I will have some investigating to do tonight. It seems like something fishy is going on at the bakery across town."

Maddie busied herself around the store for another half an hour or so just to make sure that neither Bailey nor Kyle decided to come back and check up on her. Once she knew she had waited long enough, she packed Astoria in her usual bag, grabbed her keys, and headed home.

As soon as she arrived home, she headed for the garage. She had an old clunker of a car that she hardly drove. She didn't need to, Rockcrest Cove was a pretty small town and you could get to just about any place you wanted on foot in less than 30 minutes, so cars were only for when the weather was pretty bad. She looked up the address to Evan's bakery across town and easily found the directions on her home computer. She grabbed a couple of pieces of left over fried chicken from the fridge and gave a piece to Astoria and headed for the car.

She drove by Evan's bakery and observed quite a flow of business coming in and out. Some of her old customers she hadn't seen in a while had obviously switched loyalties. Madeline parked her car about half a block away and just sat and watched. She knew what she needed to find out would be in that bakery. While she didn't know what she was looking for, she knew if she sat there long enough, she'd know it when she saw it.

CHAPTER FIVE

The bakery was finally open and as busy as ever. Madeline had been rushing about dealing with customers from the moment the doors had opened. It seemed that the news of the previous week's excitement had accomplished just the opposite: if anyone had been trying to sabotage her business, it had certainly backfired.

At the moment Madeline was in her kitchen floating from one station to another, working feverishly to fill an unusually large order for the Wilhelm Group Foundation. While the order was the biggest she had ever had for her bakery, it was certainly not something she couldn't handle. Madeline knew her recipes by heart and could easily adapt them to larger orders whenever needed.

The flow of morning customers had finally begun to slow down to a trickle, so she left Rita and Sandra to handle the few customers that came in so she could give her full attention to the order. She was relieved to be in the kitchen alone. That was when she could do her best thinking.

She barely heard the chime that alerted them that a new customer had walked in. She didn't need to, because she knew that the girls were completely capable of handling the job on their own. So she was completely startled when she heard Bailey call to her as she walked into the kitchen to greet her.

"Oh! My goodness."

Madeline reacted by putting her hand on her throat.

"My girl, you scared me out of ten years' growth!" she laughed.

They gave each other air kisses, a custom they had when Madeline was baking. That way she didn't have to stop to wash her hands before she got back to work.

"Bailey, what are you doing here? Don't you have classes today?"

"No, Gran. We're off for the holiday."

Madeline looked up briefly from her mixing. "Oh? Holiday?"

She was trying to run the calendar through her head. What day was it? She was having a hard time keeping track of all the events that were happening. It was all becoming a blur.

"Oh. Ok," she finally said.

She needed to get focused on filling her order. She had lost a lot of business while her store was closed and she couldn't afford to lose any more.

"So, what brings you by then," she said, slapping her hands together, sending a cloud of flour up into the air.

Bailey walked around the stainless steel counter so that she was facing her gran. "I had an idea," she said with a mischievous look on her face.

Maddie gave her an inquisitive look, but the rest of her body continued to work. She said nothing, but it was apparent she was waiting for more information.

"I thought that after you closed for the day"—

Bailey watched her gran to see if there was any reaction—

"The three of us, me, you, and Kyle, could try to reenact what happened the night of the murder."

Maddie's hands paused for half a second while she thought about the idea.

"Yeah, but we don't know what happened."

Bailey continued on, not letting Maddie's comment sway her. "I know. But, I've been doing a lot of research online. I've found out a lot about Emma and possible motives people may have for killing her. I thought we could play some of these out, here at the bakery."

"Hmmm," Maddie said. "I didn't know you'd been that busy. I thought you were focusing on your studies."

"Trust me, Gran, this fits right in with my studies." Bailey looked hopefully at her Gran.

"What d'you say? Want to give it a try?"

Maddie thought about it for a moment.

"What the hell," she said. "Can't hurt."

She began filling a pastry bag with some of her famous frosting and expertly piped her unique designs onto her freshly baked pastries. Bailey looked on with admiration; she couldn't fathom how she could be so artistic. The intricate little designs she made without the aid of a mold or a picture always amazed her. She reached into the empty frosting bowl and ran her finger along the rim and stuck it in her mouth, relishing its sweetness.

Maddie quickly reached out and slapped her hand, a practice she had been doing since Bailey was a small child.

"Don't do that," she chastised.

"Oh, Gran. You're already done with it," Bailey argued playfully. "You're just going to wash it all down the drain."

"Oh hush," Maddie commented and continued decorating her pastries.

"So, what time should I come back, Gran?"

"What?" Maddie had already turned her attention back to her baking.

"What time tonight should I come back?" Bailey asked again. "For the reenactments," she added.

"Oh. I think we'll close around five today."

"Kinda late, isn't it, Gran?"

"Yes, it is," she agreed. "I have a lot of work to catch up on."

"Oh, ok. I'll call Kyle to let him know."

Maddie didn't respond, and Bailey knew that was her cue to leave. It was always difficult to get her gran's attention when she was in the kitchen. It was the only place where she could totally zone out. She gave her gran an air kiss and left the room just as silently as she had arrived.

That evening, just as the sun was beginning to set, Madeline, Bailey, and Kyle sat in the office looking over Bailey's notes. The information Bailey had collected over the last couple of days was impressive.

As Kyle finished reading the last page of Bailey's notes, he looked up.

"Wow! The information you've uncovered is quite detailed," He commented.

"Are you sure your sources are reliable?"

"Well, she's certainly had a long list of enemies. Gran is not the only one who had a gripe with Emma."

"Looks like it. But how do you propose we figure all this out?"

"Well, I know she slept around, but I didn't know how far she'd go," Maddie said as she finished reading over the notes.

"Well, none of it is proof," Kyle added. "It's all circumstantial until we get some hard evidence."

"Of course," Bailey agreed, "but we have to start somewhere. Someone was angry enough to kill her. Maybe it's someone on this list."

"Ok. Where do you think we should start?" Kyle asked, not really believing that the reenactments would lead anywhere.

"Well, I think we should start with this one." She reached over and grabbed an index card off the table.

"I call this one," she said playfully, "Emma and the Mayor." She teasingly waved the card in front of Kyle.

Kyle grabbed the card from her. "Really?" He looked intrigued.

Madeline got up from her seat. "Why don't you two get started? I need to finish up a few things in the kitchen first."

"Oh, Gran. We need you," Bailey whined.

"I'll join you later," Madeline assured her. "But I need to finish up an order in the kitchen before I close up for the night."

"Can't you get the girls to do that?"

"I sent the girls home already. They'd been here since five this morning."

"Yeah, but—"

"Listen. If you let me do this, I'll be all yours for the rest of the evening."

"But I thought I could play the part of the different people that hate Emma. I think that'd be fun, and you could play Emma."

"I will, as soon as I finish my work. I don't want to be here too late after what happened."

Bailey couldn't argue with that point. Within minutes, the sound of scuffling noises coming from the kitchen somehow soothed Bailey and gave her the assurance that her gran was in fact ok. She knew that when she was stressed she always buried herself in the kitchen, baking all sorts of delectable goodies. It was a wonder that Bailey didn't grow up with more of a cushion around her middle than she already had. She enjoyed eating her gran's treats just as much as she knew her gran enjoyed baking them.

She turned and gave Kyle a quiet look.

"Well, I guess that's it," Kyle said. "We might as well call it a night."

"Why?" Bailey asked innocently. "We can still do a little reenactment with just you and me."

"How?" Kyle asked. "Your gran is in the kitchen and there's no one else here."

Bailey leaned across the desk, a little closer to Kyle than usual. She threw him a coquettish look and gave him an innocent little school-girl pout.

"You're here."

"Well, yeah, but."

"You can play Emma."

Kyle stared at her for half a beat while the thought registered in his mind. His hands flew up in front of him as if to ward off a threat.

"Oh, no," he said, and began backing up toward the door."

"Oh come on, Kyle. It could be fun."

"For who?" he asked. "Certainly not me."

"Why not?" Bailey persisted. She had a very persuasive way about her.

"No," he protested again, more firmly this time. "Absolutely not."

"Kyle. Don't you want to figure out who the murderer is? Get my gran off the hook?" She tried another flirtatious approach.

"Of course," he defended. "But how is my playing a woman going to do that?"

"You're not playing the woman," she said. "You're playing the victim."

"Oh, my mistake," he countered.

"What's wrong with you?" she demanded, switching characters again.

Kyle looked genuinely perplexed and confused. He'd never seen Bailey switch personas like that before. He gave a little half smile. She was turning out to be more interesting than he had thought.

In the kitchen, Madeline was deep in thought, thinking about all the information Bailey had found out about Emma. She was surprised by what she had learned, but not completely. Knowing Emma as long as she had, she always knew that there was something beneath the surface. Still, even knowing the uglier side of the woman, she would have never wished anything bad on her; certainly not this. She looked up at the back door of the shop and wondered once again, who was the real killer? She wanted to find the murderer as much for Emma as she did for herself.

Across the hall, she could hear Bailey and Kyle laughing as they were trying to role play what could have happened on that dreadful night. She felt a little guilty about the laughter, but at the same time she realized that none of them had laughed since that horrible day, and it felt good to relieve some of the tensions that had built up since then. She decided to bake some cupcakes to keep the evening light. No one could resist her cupcakes, she thought, reaching down for her special cupcake tins.

After lining them up on the counter, she started rooting around in the cabinets for her ingredients. As was her usual habit while she worked, she began talking to herself.

"Ok. Now. I have the flour, sugar, and butter, lemon extract...let's see. Oh, I need the baking powder."

She reached up and grabbed it. "Oh, the eggs." She went into the large walk-in refrigerator and came out with eggs, milk, and."

"Now," she said, "for my secret ingredient."

She grabbed a footstool and pulled it up in front of the tall shelving unit, climbed on top, and began to reach for her special powder. No one knew what the combination of ingredients was that she always included in her recipes. She hadn't even told Bailey what she put in them, although Bailey never really cared. She was just happy to have them whenever she wanted them.

As she grabbed the container and slid it off the shelf, something fell from underneath. It was so fast, Madeline barely noticed it, but she did hear the soft thud as it hit the floor. She climbed down from her stool, placed the canister on the counter, and stooped down to pick up a small red notebook.

"What's this?" she said to herself.

Turning the pages, Emma's characteristic handwriting with her distinctive slanting and the curling of letters that shouldn't be curled was apparent. Emma always was one to go against the grain. It didn't take long to notice that nearly every page had notes about one of Maddie's secret recipes on it. Other pages had scribbling marks she couldn't decipher. It was apparent that Emma had been trying to copy her recipes, and had kept a record of everything Madeline had been doing since she had started working for her.

Madeline crunched up her eyebrows in a perplexing way. She looked through the pages and tried to figure out what all of it meant. Slowly, she began to remember.

Chapter Six

There was something about the notebook that seemed strange but familiar at the same time. As Madeline flipped through the pages, she noticed that Emma had made extensive notes on the very recipes that had made her bakery so popular. Recipes she had never shared with anyone, even Bailey, were being analyzed and tested to see if Emma could figure out the recipes. The strangest thing she found was a page with newer recipes that she was working on and new ideas she hadn't even tested yet.

This notebook was new, but Emma hadn't been working for her for more than two years. Who could have left it in the kitchen, and how could Emma have found out about it? Better yet, how is it that the police missed it when they went through her entire store just a few days ago? Madeline looked genuinely perplexed as she leaned on the stainless steel kitchen counter and flipped through the notebook's tattered pages. A little anger was beginning to boil up inside her, and she regretted that she had ever hired Emma and brought her into her confidence. Her mind drifted back to the moment she realized Emma was not the true friend she had always believed her to be, the day the veil of innocence was lifted and she finally saw what everyone else had seen.

~~~

It was two years ago and Madeline's store had grown fast. From its very beginning, her new pastry recipes were a big hit. She was relishing in her glory; the business was doing well and she had just gotten a great review in the local paper. The store had become so busy that Madeline was barely able to keep up with the customer demand. Instead of working in the back office taking care of administrative duties, she had had to put her paperwork down and help the girls in the front to keep up with the steady flow of traffic during the morning rush.

Madeline ran her forearm across the brow of her forehead and gazed at the growing line of customers. She had mixed feelings at the sight. On the one hand, she was thrilled to see so many customers and she relished in her business's success, but on the other hand, she was tired and frustrated. She began to doubt herself and question her ability to run a successful business. It was far more work than she had anticipated.

"May I help the next in line, please?" she announced to the crowd.

A stoutly business woman stepped up to the counter. "I'd like a dozen crescent rolls, please."

"Sure thing."

Madeline looked in the display case to see that the crescent rolls were nearly all gone. There were only two remaining.

"I'm sorry, we only have two left. If you don't mind waiting a moment, there'll be more coming from the kitchen soon."

"Oh, great!" the woman said with relief. "I was worried that you were going to tell me you were out. I don't mind waiting."

"Thank you," Madeline said. "How would you like a free cup of coffee while you wait? It shouldn't take long."

"Thank you," the woman said appreciatively. She gracefully accepted the coffee and took a seat at a nearby table.

Madeline turned to Emma, who had been helping her during the rush.

"Emma, could you go in the back and ask Rita to bring out some more crescent rolls?"

"Sure thing," Emma said and disappeared through the door leading to the back office.

Madeline immediately turned to help the next customer in line. But after she had helped three more customers, neither Emma nor Rita had returned. Relieved, she noticed that the morning rush was just about over. The line was beginning to thin out.

Rita appeared from the kitchen, her apron dusty with a spray of flour and her hands caked with wet dough. She carried a tray of crescent rolls and handed them to Madeline before turning to retreat back to the kitchen.

"Where's Emma?" Madeline asked.

"I don't know. She's not out here?"

"No."

"Hmm," Madeline wondered out loud.

"She just came in and said you needed these and then left," Rita offered. "I thought she had come back out here to help."

Madeline looked at the two girls. "Do you two think you can handle it now?"

"Yes, ma'am," they both agreed.

Madeline took off her apron and pushed through the door to the back. She checked the kitchen but Emma was nowhere to be found. As she walked past her office door, she could hear Emma's voice.

Who was she talking to? She wondered.

She almost disregarded it and went back to the front, but then she heard Emma's voice again.

"Yes. I have some of the recipes but not all of them."

There was silence while the person on the other end spoke.

"Yes, that's right," Emma said. "But I haven't figured out the combination yet."

Another pause.

"It's a blend of some sort. She mixes it and brings it in. I don't even know where she buys the stuff, let alone what it is."

Convinced that Emma was sharing her secret recipes, she pushed through the doorway to find her sitting quite comfortably in her chair, her feet on the desk and her back to the door. She was flipping through some small little book. Maybe it was the same one Maddie was holding now.

"Yes, that's right." She was nodding.

Emma paused while the other person spoke.

"Mmm hmm," she said into the phone. "Maybe we can get some and have it analyzed at a lab or something." Laughter.

"Emma!" Madeline shouted.

Startled, Emma visibly jumped at the sound of Madeline's voice. She turned to see Madeline standing there, who was aghast at what she had just heard.

"What are you doing?" Madeline demanded.

"Um, ah, I was just talking to…"

"To who?" Madeline said harshly. It took a lot for her to get angry, but when she did, she had a fury like no other. She was almost at that point now.

"Uh, to my brother," Emma recovered. "He just wanted to know what's so special about your pastries."

"And you told him my secret?"

"Well, I didn't think it would cause any harm. I mean, he doesn't even know how to cook or anything? He's just curious." She was scrambling hard to think of a way to wiggle out of this one.

"A lab?" Madeline questioned. "That doesn't sound very innocent to me."

"Oh," Emma said with a nervous laugh. "We were just kidding. I told him how secretive you were about your recipes, and he said maybe we should get a lab to figure out your secret ingredient." She laughed a little more until she noticed that Madeline wasn't laughing along with her. "Anyway, what harm can it do? You don't share your secrets with anyone. Not even me."

Madeline stood there trying to decide exactly what to do. She debated whether Emma was telling the truth or not. Her instincts were telling her to fire her on the spot, but she knew Emma would not take it well, and right now she didn't need the negative attention that firing her would undoubtedly bring. Rockcrest Cove was still a small town, and all her newfound prosperity could be destroyed with just one wrong decision. But she was still pretty angry that Emma would give out something so valuable so easily.

"Listen, Emma. These secrets are the heart of my business. I told you on day one that I don't share this information with anyone, not even my own family."

"Yeah, I know." Emma tried to sound apologetic. "I just didn't think it would be that big a deal. I mean it was only one recipe."

"If I catch you sharing information like this again, Emma"—Madeline spoke with a forcefulness that Emma had never seen before—"you're fired."

Emma stood there, her apologetic face slowly giving way to anger.

Madeline watched a full transformation happen right before her eyes. For a moment the two women stood staring at each other.

There was no way for Emma to hold it in any longer. "How dare you."

Madeline looked nonplussed at the statement, clearly taken off guard. "I beg your pardon?" she queried.

"You heard me," Emma said. Her anger and jealousy had finally got the better of her.

"How dare you sit here in your precious little domain and treat me as though I had absolutely nothing to do with your success. As if you did it all by yourself."

"What are you talking about?"

"I'm talking about this store. How you cheated to get this store," she said.

"I've worked this store from its very beginning with my own hands, with my own sweat."

"And where did you get the money?" Emma demanded.

"The money?" Madeline looked confused.

"Yes, the money," Emma said. "You used the money you won from the competition that the three of us entered."

Madeline thought for a moment. She needed a minute to process the information Emma was spewing at her.

"Yes, I used the money from the competition that I won," she said, putting a strong emphasis on the "I."

"You should've shared the money with us."

"What? Whatever gave you the idea that you deserved part of my winnings?"

"We entered the contest together."

"Yes, we did. But you and Evan pulled out and decided to compete on your own."

"But you used our recipe."

"I most certainly did not." Madeline was aghast. "I used my own recipe."

"We had all agreed on the praline cupcake for the entry, and that's what you won with."

"Well, it wasn't your recipe. You took yours when you pulled out of the team," Madeline defended.

Now furious at the accusation, she continued. "And I'm going to say it again. If I ever catch you sharing my recipes with anyone ever again, I will fire you."

"The day you fire me is the day I go public and tell the world how you cheated in the competition and bribed your way to success." Emma's voice spewed icy venom in Madeline's direction.

"Well, then," Madeline said with icy calmness. "Let that day be today." She pointed in the direction of the front door. "Get out of my store."

Emma looked shocked. She never really thought Madeline would actually fire her. She stood there still as a statue, her eyes red from anger.

"You'll regret this," Emma responded, but with less fire than she had before.

Madeline stood there, cold, angry, bitter, and deeply hurt. All this time she had thought that Emma was her friend, and now she saw her for who she really was. Emma grabbed her bag and stormed out of the store. She tried to slam the door as she left, but the electric device that allowed it to open and close slowly wouldn't let her. She only made herself look more ridiculous as the other customers stared on. Humiliated, she left the store.

Standing in the office, Madeline worked hard to regain her composure. She picked up Astoria and stroked her soft fur to calm her nerves while she paced back and forth. Her thoughts were all over the place.

How long had Emma been giving away her secrets?

Who was she giving them to?

Why was she so convinced that she had cheated in the competition?

The questions wouldn't stop running through her mind. Was she such a poor judge of character?

Why hadn't she seen Emma for who she really was?

It took nearly an hour for her to calm herself down so she could get back to work. After a while she went into the kitchen to do what she did best. Bake. She had several orders she needed to fill before the day was over, so she'd better get to it. Both Rita and Sandra had heard the argument between the two women and thought it better to stay in the front of the store for a while. They both exchanged glances as Madeline entered the room and went to the register and started looking at the order slips.

"Rita," Madeline said. "Where is that large order for 300 cupcakes we took yesterday?"

"It's done," she said.

"Done?"

"Yes." She pointed over at a bunch of boxes all wrapped up and ready for customer pick up.

"Emma did them this morning."

Madeline looked at the boxes and her anger began to rise again. "Oh," she said, and went and picked up the boxes to take them to the back of the store.

Rita started to speak but thought better of it. She had never seen Madeline so angry and wasn't sure how far she should go.

Madeline grabbed the boxes and headed straight for the back door, her composure in check but her anger still strong. She had just learned that Emma was not who she presented herself to be, and she didn't want her doing anything as important as filling a customer's order. She opened the dumpster and dumped a full box of cupcakes in just as Bailey walked behind her.

"Gran!" Bailey spoke with alarm. "What are you doing?"

"I'm so mad," Madeline shouted.

Her whole body trembled as she reached for another box.

"I'm so mad, I could scream."

She took a second box and with one big gesture dumped another full box of cupcakes into the dumpster. She barely noticed Bailey as she reached for a third box until she felt the firm but gentle tug on her arm. She turned and saw Bailey holding her arm, a look of sincere concern spread across her face.

"What's wrong, Gran?" she asked. "What happened? Why are you throwing away perfectly good cupcakes?"

"It's Emma," Madeline finally explained. "I don't want anything she's ever done associated with my store."

"Gran!" Bailey said, perplexed. "What could she have done to get you so angry?"

"She's been giving away my recipes," Madeline shouted.

Bailey was speechless for a moment. "What? To who?"

"I don't know," Madeline said, finally beginning to calm herself.

"She said it was to her brother, but I'm not so sure. I walked into the office and heard her talking on the phone to someone."

"Are you serious?" Bailey asked incredulously.

"Yes, I'm serious."

Bailey took a step backward, her mind reeling. "How could she do that? Why would she do that?"

"She says that I cheated in the competition years ago. And that's why I won." Madeline started pacing back and forth. She felt as if she would explode.

Bailey raised her hands in front of her in a hold-on-a-minute gesture while Madeline reached for another box of cupcakes.

"Hold on a minute, Gran," she said.

"Just hold on a minute."

She stood there trying to think of something as she watched her gran dump another box of cupcakes into the dumpster.

Bailey said nothing in response to the last statement. "Where is she?" she asked.

"I don't know. I fired her."

"Good for you, Gran. Good for you."

Madeline took a long, hard sigh as she began to regain her composure once again. With each dump of cupcakes, it was like she was riding herself of a little more of Emma. By the time the last box was dumped, she felt almost like her old self again.

"If you don't mind, Bailey, I have a large order to fill."

Madeline wiped her hands on her apron and turned to face her granddaughter. She suddenly appeared the picture of calm.

Bailey stood stunned, looking at her grandmother. She had never seen her that angry ever, and she wasn't quite sure what to think of it.

"Are you ok?" she asked.

"I'm perfectly fine," Madeline responded. "I just have a lot of work to do." She walked away, leaving Bailey standing alone in stunned silence.

Bailey drove home, incredulous due to the events that had just transpired. She was appalled that Emma would do such a thing to her gran after all she had done for her.

Rockcrest Cove had high and low peaks of activity throughout the day. The early morning rush before people headed off to work was usually the busiest time for everyone. Afterward, there was a lull in activity until the lunchtime crowd began to break away for a fast hour of eating before rushing back to their work stations.

It was during that lull that Bailey found herself driving the streets of Rockcrest Cove, trying to decide what to do. She knew she had to get to the bottom of everything before anything could be resolved. She thought if she could find Emma and talk to her, she could get a reasonable explanation for what had happened. She knew Emma well enough to know her usual haunts and decided to try to go and find her. Sure enough, she saw Emma's car parked on the road alongside Rockcrest Cove's central park. She pulled up alongside Emma's car and got out.

Standing next to her car, she shielded her eyes from the bright sunlight, looking for places that Emma might be. There was a concession stand in the middle of the park that seemed as good a place to start as any.

Emma was sitting on a bench near the stand, sipping what appeared to be a cup of coffee. She seemed to be casually chatting on her cell phone as Bailey approached. To her surprise, she saw a smile spread across Emma's face and heard laughter emerge from the woman. Bailey's sense of reason left her at that point. She could only think of her gran and how upset she was, and this woman was making a mockery of her. Without thinking, Bailey approached Emma and swiftly snatched the phone out of her hand mid-sentence.

"What!" Emma leaped from her seat. "I was in the middle of a conversation," she protested.

"To the same person you gave my grandmother's recipes to?" Bailey challenged.

Emma looked at the younger woman and started to say something, but then she thought better of it.

"What were you thinking sharing my gran's baking secrets?"

Emma took an indignant stance. "Like you care," she said. "You're hardly ever around anyway."

Bailey refused to take the bait. "How dare you try to sabotage her business!"

"It's not her business. It should've been our business. But she's so greedy and selfish."

"Selfish!" Bailey looked at her, eyes wide. "Selfish!" she repeated. "Who's the one trying to steal her secrets and sell them to the highest bidder?'

"What are you talking about? I was just trying to take back what was mine. Your grandmother stole those recipes from me."

"What recipes?"

"She took my recipe and used it for the competition, and then when she won, she used her winnings to open up that bakery." Emma stuck her chest out in a subconscious effort to appear bigger, her arms thrown back in a confrontational stance.

"She never stole your recipes. That's just some idea you cooked up because you were jealous of her success," Bailey retorted. She was not about to back down.

Soon, a crowd began to notice the heated exchange.

"That's what she told you."

"That's what I know."

"And how would you know that? You're still wet behind the ears."

"You want to know how I know?" Bailey stuck her finger in Emma's face.

"You want to know how I know?"

She paused to catch her breath for just a second.

"Because, if she had stolen your recipes for her bakery, you wouldn't have had to sneak around and steal them."

The words hit Emma like a slap in the face. The argument was sound, and Emma had no defense for the accusation, so she changed tactics.

"Well, you shouldn't have been surprised," she finally said. "After all, the espionage thing was your idea."

Bailey looked as if she had been physically struck. "Are you deranged? Are you out of your mind?" she asked.

"There is no possible way that I would have done anything to damage my grandmother's reputation."

"Of course not," Emma agreed, seeing that her words had hit their mark.

"It's just that you yourself said that sometimes it is necessary to do some undercover work in order to get to the bottom of some cases."

Bailey, recalling that conversation, knew that Emma had taken her comments entirely out of context. She had simply been talking about investigating legal cases in which the proof was not always so easy to find. She decided to not give her the satisfaction of debating such a ridiculous issue with her.

"My grandmother did everything to give you a helping hand, even offered to help you win the competition. And this is how you repay her?"

Emma looked on as Bailey stood there, fists clenched, eyes piercing into her soul like daggers cutting through her flesh. She was trying to find a way to respond to the statements, but nothing was coming to mind.

"I promise you this, Emma," Bailey said. "After what you've done, I wouldn't ever advise you to enter another competition here in Rockcrest Cove for as long as you live."

"And how would you stop me?"

"I'm pretty darn close to finishing my law degree. I guarantee you that I have learned quite a few ways to stop you." Bailey spat out the last words and turned on her heel, only then realizing that she still held Emma's phone in her hand.

"My phone, please," Emma said, her hand out.

"Oh, this is your phone?" Bailey asked, turning the device over in her hands.

"You know it is."

Bailey turned and tossed the phone into the lake as she walked away.

"Maybe you should try to do a little espionage to find out where it is," she responded.

CHAPTER SEVEN

Madeline snapped out of her thoughts as if she had been struck in the head. It was clear that Emma's sneaky practices had not been stopped the day she was fired. As a matter of fact, it appeared that it had escalated from then on. She had noticed a decline in her business, but she did not connect it to Emma since the woman had not been in her store for at least two years. At least as far as she knew, Emma had left on that awful day. Now, she realized that Emma must've had an accomplice to help steal her secrets.

The fact that the door was open the night she found her meant that Emma and someone else had had access to her shop after hours. Who knows what information they had been able to collect all those years.

Bailey and Kyle were still in the other room play acting. Madeline quickly forgot about the cupcakes and crossed the hall to show them the book. As she entered the room, Bailey and Kyle, who had a makeshift handbag on his arm, both burst into giggles, but the laughter didn't last long. As soon as they saw her face, they realized something had happened.

"What's wrong, Gran?"

Madeline held up the little red notebook and tossed it onto the table. "I found this."

"What is it?" Bailey asked as she picked up the notebook and examined it.

"It looks like a book of a bunch of my recipes that Emma had collected over the years."

"Are you serious?" Kyle said as he reached over and grabbed the book from Bailey. He flipped through the pages as if looking for something to jump out at him.

"It appears that Emma did not stop stealing from me the day I fired her two years ago," Madeline said.

"Obviously," Bailey agreed.

"Apparently she's been coming in and out of my store all along, going through my things and stealing whatever information she could."

"But how was she able to get in?" Bailey asked. "Someone had to have been helping her."

"Maybe she had an extra key made," Madeline suggested.

"Do you think one of the girls could've been helping her?"

"No. I don't think so. They never could stand Emma, and Emma never made it any secret that she didn't like them at all."

"Well, someone had to have been helping her these last two years."

The two women tossed ideas back and forth, trying to figure out how Emma could have worked behind the scenes to steal Madeline's secrets. Kyle, on the other hand, was deep in thought.

"This can't be right," he finally interjected.

Both women looked as if they had forgotten he was in the room.

He continued. "This can't be right. Something's wrong here."

"What d'you mean?" Bailey asked.

"Well, think about it. The police were in here for three days, examining every inch of this place. They even locked you out, Madeline."

"Yeah," she agreed.

"So, why didn't they find this notebook then?"

The women had no answer to the question, but it did inspire deeper thought.

"You mean to tell me that with all those police investigators running in and out of your store, with access to every part of it, this little book was not found?"

"So, what are you saying, Kyle?" Madeline asked.

"I think this book is a plant."

"Yeah, but it has so many of my secret recipes, even the new ones I was developing."

"I don't doubt that Emma had devised a way to get in and steal your secrets, but even she wouldn't have been so foolish as to leave her book behind for you to find."

"So, what are you implying?" Bailey asked this time.

"It's a way to incriminate you, Madeline."

Both women looked stunned. The thought had never occurred to them that someone could be trying to incriminate Madeline in Emma's murder.

"Think about it," Kyle tried to explain.

"The murder takes place at your place of business, the victim is a long-time rival of yours, and the evidence is found hidden away in your kitchen. All the incriminating evidence is pointing at you."

"So, are you saying that someone snuck in here after the police investigated to plant this in my kitchen?"

"I'd bet money on it," Kyle confirmed.

"Someone doesn't want us to look at other possibilities for why Emma may have been killed. They want us to focus on this rivalry of yours instead."

The three of them stood in silence, pondering the logic that Kyle had put before them. It was a logical conclusion, and it was disturbing that someone would want to set Madeline up for murder. How desperate could they be?

"Bailey, you said you uncovered a list of other reasons why someone would want to kill Emma."

"Yeah," she said, and reached to pull out her own notebook.

"Did you know that Emma was caught in a tryst with one of her professors at your culinary school?" Bailey asked Madeline.

"What?" Madeline was stunned.

"But that's small potatoes compared to this one."

Bailey held up a single page for them all to see. "It seems that Emma had an affair with Mayor Bryson."

No one spoke, so she continued. "It was all swept under the rug because it was an election year. It seems like when the mayor wanted to break it off, Emma threatened to go public. Money changed hands and everything went silent."

"How do you know all of this?" Kyle asked.

"I just put out a few choice words with the local gossipers. They know everything. Rockcrest Cove is a small town; there is no such thing as a secret in a town like this. Somebody, somewhere, always knows something. I went on several chat lines, checked up with people on Facebook, LinkedIn, and other social media sites. Now that Emma's dead, you'd be surprised by how many people want to talk."

"So, how do we proceed?" Madeline finally spoke up.

"I think we should start at the top," Bailey said. "Let's go see Kelsey Bryson."

"I don't think that's a good idea," Kyle said.

"Why not?"

"If the murderer is trying to divert attention away from him, two amateur investigators will just stir up a hornet's nest."

"In the meantime, I have Chief Nolan compiling a whole hornet's nest just for me," Madeline put in.

"If I don't find another suspect, I'm in a lot of trouble."

Kyle thought for a moment. He knew that if he turned in the notebook, Nolan would use it as evidence against Madeline, but if they held onto it and said nothing, it would look even more incriminating.

"We need more evidence," he finally said. "We need to find out what really happened between Emma and Mayor Bryson."

"Then it's settled," Bailey said.

"Gran and I will go to see Kelsey, but we'll do it on the quiet. That way, if it turns out to be nothing, we'll be in the clear."

The drive to the Bryson's home was a short one, but it felt as if they had traveled to a new world. On their side of town, the neighborhoods consisted of small family cottages and multi-unit apartment buildings, but here on this side of Rockcrest Cove, they were driving past the stately mansions of the upper echelon. The mayor had been a prominent figure in Rockcrest Cove for quite a few years.

Madeline and Bailey were a bit awe struck when the saw the house. Not quite a palatial mansion like others in the immediate area, but certainly a cut well above what either of the ladies were accustomed to. The driveway to the house was a horseshoe affair, where you entered through one gate, which led you right to the front steps of the Bryson home, and exited through another.

They rode in Bailey's car since Madeline's would not have been able to blend into the surroundings without drawing undue attention. Bailey's car wasn't much better, but at least it was a newer model and it had a decent paint job. The two women pulled up to the front steps and were immediately greeted by one of the Bryson's servants, who opened the door and escorted them up the steps. Neither of them were surprised. It stood to reason that no one would have been able to traverse that drive without being seen, even if their visit was unannounced.

"Who shall I say is calling?" the servant asked.

"Madeline McDougal to see Mrs. Bryson."

"Please wait in here." The servant gestured with his hand into a small room off the hallway.

The two ladies followed his lead and found a quaint little sitting room that was quite comfortable. Before long, Kelsey Bryson appeared in the doorway, a hint of confusion on her face.

"Hello," she said as she floated into the room.

"Mrs. Bryson," Madeline started, extending her hand, "it's so good to see you again."

Kelsey looked even more perplexed. "I'm sorry. Have we met?"

"Oh, you probably don't remember me. It was so long ago, and only for a brief moment," Madeline explained.

"You were at the grand opening of my bakery ten years ago."

Kelsey gave Madeline a once over. "Oh, yes," she replied.

"That was quite an opening you had. Businesses all over have been trying to match that big affair."

"Well, it was a special occasion for me, that's for sure," Madeline agreed. "I had wanted my own bakery for years."

"Well, you did well for yourself," Kelsey praised.

"But what brings you here today?" she asked, anxious to get to the point.

"Well, I'm afraid it's a rather delicate situation," Madeline commented. After a short hesitation, she continued.

"I'm sure you've heard about what happened to Emma Larson."

"Oh," Kelsey stated, almost as if someone had let the air out of her.

"Yes, I did. A sad affair, but I can't say that I'm surprised," she added.

Both Madeline and Bailey looked up but didn't say anything.

"Can I get you ladies something to drink? Coffee? Tea? It's been so long since I've had any visitors around. I could use the company."

They all settled down to a little small talk before the conversation got back around to Emma.

"Kelsey," Madeline started, "do you mind if I ask you a personal question?"

Kelsey put her cup down on the table and turned to face Madeline. "About Emma?"

"Yes."

Madeline put her cup down and faced the other woman. "As you've probably heard, there was no love lost between me and Emma, and we had a serious falling out a couple of years back. We hadn't spoken to each other since."

"Well, news travels here in Rockcrest Cove," Kelsey agreed.

"My guess is you're here because you've heard the rumors about Emma and my husband."

"Yes, we have." Bailey finally spoke for the first time.

"Well, I have to admit, there was no love lost between me and Emma either."

Kelsey looked pensive as she recalled that day several years ago.

"I'm not going to lie. When I heard what happened, I wasn't at all shocked, nor was I the least bit saddened. The woman nearly wrecked my marriage."

"So the rumors were true?" Bailey asked.

"Without a doubt." Kelsey turned so she could look Madeline directly in the face. She leaned in a little.

"As a matter of fact, Madeline, the whole affair was your fault."

"Me? How could I be responsible? I never put Emma and your husband together."

Her defensive posture was understandable. First, she was accused of murdering her long-time rival, and now she was being accused of setting up an adulterous affair.

"Oh, let me explain myself," Kelsey offered.

"I didn't mean it was you directly that set up the affair, but it was your praline cupcakes," she explained.

"Ever since your bakery opened, my husband couldn't get enough of your pralines. Every time we had an event, he had to place a large order with your bakery. You are the only one that can make them, you know."

'Yes, I know," Madeline said with a little relief.

"Well, I always thought it was the cupcakes that he loved, so I never questioned why he wanted to order them all the time."

Kelsey paused for a minute while she tried to recall the events of that day so long ago. Even years later, her emotions were still raw.

"I didn't know anything, as I was busy, involved in my own projects as the wife of the mayor."

"I see," Madeline said. She felt she had to interject something, but she really wanted the lady to continue on without interruption.

"Anyway, I was often out during the day, going to my different events, but on that day, I had forgotten my calendar, so I had to return home to pick it up. That's when I found them."

Bailey gasped. "You found them?"

"Yes. Upstairs in our bedroom." She rounded on Madeline.

"With your cupcakes all over our bed. They didn't even have enough sense to use a guest bedroom, where they were less likely to be caught."

Madeline was mortified. She had allowed Emma to make deliveries for several of her clients before. Could she have done this with any of her other clients as well?

"I'm so sorry, Kelsey," Madeline said. "Emma made a lot of deliveries for me. I never thought about the possibilities."

"Well, it backfired on my husband," Kelsey continued.

"He thought he had caught himself a young little filly he could keep on the side, but it turned out she only wanted the affair as a way to exploit the relationship and get money out of him."

She took a deep breath before she continued. "I was furious, and I wanted a divorce right then and there. Tom was afraid that a divorce would ruin his chances at reelection, so he decided to get rid of her instead."

"So, what did he do?"

"That's when her true colors came out." Kelsey spoke now with bitterness and anger in her voice.

"She threatened to expose him and do a full exposé in the local paper. Tom ended up having to pay a lot of money to keep her quiet. It took a lot of lawyers and hard-core negotiating to keep things quiet."

"Oh my! I had no idea," Madeline said again, stunned.

"Oh, you don't know the half of it," Kelsey continued.

"Where do you think she got the money to get that new bakery off the ground? Emma had no money, and her partner, Evan, he had even less."

"She couldn't qualify for any type of bank loan, so she did what she did best." Kelsey stopped to get a little more control of her voice before she continued.

"She started doing the same thing to a whole host of people. Martin, the president of First Allied Bank, Allen, the owner of Barclay's Investments, Peter, president of Constance Property Management—"

"Wait," Bailey interrupted. "Are you telling me she did the same thing with all of these men?"

"Yes," Kelsey confirmed.

"And more. That's how she made the money to get that rival bakery off the ground."

"She was clever, that one. I knew that one day, she'd get it in the end."

CHAPTER EIGHT

Madeline and Bailey drove out of the Kelsey's driveway, speechless. While they expected to uncover some of Emma's secrets, they didn't expect the earful they had gotten. If Kelsey's accusations proved true, there could be a host of possible suspects who had wanted to see Emma eliminated. But there was a nagging bit of doubt running through their minds.

Hell hath no fury like a woman scorned, and it was clear there was no woman more bitter than Kelsey Bryson.

Still, as they discussed the details of their afternoon with Kelsey, there seemed to be one continuous thread that ran through all the evidence they had uncovered so far: the rival bakery on the other side of town was the one thing that linked everything else together.

From what Madeline remembered, Evan Foster was a relatively simple man. He was neither outspoken nor pushy. Yes, he had his own ideals and dreams, as did everyone else in the school, but he was rather mousy for a man.

"Well, what do you think?" Bailey spoke up first.

"I'm not entirely sure what to think," Madeline answered.

"Do you think you can believe what Kelsey said about Emma and all of those men?"

"I'm not sure. It's a might convenient that all of this comes out after her death."

"Well, I believe it," Bailey asserted.

"I mean, she's been around the block, there's no secret about that. She's shrewd and conniving. You know that for yourself."

"Yeah, but that doesn't mean that she got into bed with all of those men."

"Think of it this way, Gran. If she slept with even half of the men Kelsey commented on and then blackmailed them into backing her business with Evan, it creates a lot more possible suspects. That could be enough to take some of the heat off of you."

"True," Madeline said, thinking about the possibilities. "But all of these things supposedly happened several years ago. Why would they wait until now to try to kill her?"

"Good point," Bailey said. "But I did find out a lot about her from those social media sites. She wasn't a very popular woman."

"Everybody knows that," Madeline continued.

"But Emma didn't just get that way recently. She's been that way her whole life. Why would anyone try to kill her now?

It doesn't make any sense." Madeline thought for minute. "Something must've happened recently to change things."

"Maybe we should talk to Kyle about this," Bailey suggested.

"Of course," Madeline agreed. "But there's something we need to do first."

Bailey strongly objected to the suggestion that they go to visit Evan and Emma's bakery across town. It seemed like a foolish and risky step that could turn out to be nothing but trouble.

"Think about it," Madeline tried to explain.

"That bakery is at the heart of everything we've uncovered so far." She began to count off the connections on her fingers.

"One, she and Evan were secret partners in this bakery while she was working for me. Two, she blackmailed Bryson to get the money to finance the bakery. Three, she was clearly stealing my recipes to give to Evan. Four, they were trying to sabotage my business and steal my customers away."

"Ok. Ok. I get it," Bailey said.

"I'm just worried that if Evan is behind it all, it's not going to sit well with him if we just walk in there like regular customers."

"Well, there's only one way to find out," Madeline said. "Turn the wheel."

"Now, Gran, let's think this through a bit more."

"Turn the wheel, Bailey."

"But wait a minute."

"Turn the wheel, Bailey."

"Yes, but—"

"Bailey! Turn the wheel," Madeline insisted.

Bailey reluctantly did as she was instructed and turned the wheel. "I think," she said, trying to get her gran to see a little reason,

"I think we should call Kyle and let him know what we're doing."

"We can talk to Kyle later," Madeline said.

She knew if Bailey spoke to him, there was a good chance he would talk her out of it. What would Evan do? She thought to herself. It was the middle of the day. If he were going to try something, he would do it much later.

They parked outside The Baker's Cup for about thirty minutes, watching a brisk business go in and out. She could see why her business had seen a drop in customers recently. Again, she watched as many of her former customers went in and out of the establishment. Obviously the new business had somehow lured them away.

"Let's go," Madeline said, and she jumped out of the car.

"Wait!" Bailey said. "Not so fast." She got out, but not nearly as fast as Madeline had. "Gran. Are you sure you want to do this?"

"Yes," Madeline said with a little irritation in her voice.

"Then we need a cover story. We can't just walk in there."

"Of course we can," Madeline said.

"It's the only way we can go in. I can't go on any pretense; Evan and I went to school together. He'll see right through any scenario we might make up."

Bailey was still not sure about entering a rival shop so openly, but she followed her gran anyway.

They entered to a busy and brisk business. Customers were happily chatting away at different booths, sipping their coffee and discussing whatever was on their mind. Unlike at Madeline's shop, where business came and went in spurts, this shop seemed to have a steady flow of traffic, and business was booming.

The plan was to enter as customers, but that idea went out the window as soon as they entered the door. Evan immediately recognized Madeline almost as soon as they arrived.

"Maddie!" he exclaimed, appearing genuinely happy to see her.

"What a pleasure it is to see you in my shop!"

He came over and gave her a great big hug, catching her completely off guard. "What brings you to my neck of the woods?" he asked jovially.

"Well, I just heard how well you were doing and decided to come check it out."

"Great! That's awesome," he said excitedly. He directed them to a corner booth.

"Why don't you have a seat and I'll be right back." He walked a few feet away from them and then turned back.

"Order whatever you want," he said.

"On the house." And then he disappeared into the crowd.

"Doesn't seem like someone who was out to run you out of business," Bailey observed.

"I'm inclined to agree with you."

The two women sat across from each other and observed the goings on in the small bakery.

Bailey was the first to speak. "Gran, do you see..." she pointed to the menu card. "These are all your specialties."

"I see that."

"And look!" Bailey pointed at the table decorations. "These are yours too."

Evan returned quickly with a couple plates of praline cupcakes. He placed them on the table in front of the women.

"My specialty," he said proudly.

Madeline looked at the cupcakes before her. This was her specialty. How did Evan get ahold of it? She wondered. As she looked around the shop, it was clear Evan's place was simply a copy of her own.

"Oh, Evan," Madeline spoke up. "I don't believe you've met my granddaughter, Bailey."

Evan turned to face Bailey and offered his hand. "Nice to meet you, Bailey."

"Nice to meet you too," Bailey responded. "This is quite a business you have here."

"Oh!" he responded enthusiastically. "I'd love to show you around," he offered.

"You know, I have your grandmother to thank for my success."

"Oh really," Bailey responded, intrigued by his enthusiasm and seeming innocence.

"How so?"

Evan slid into the seat next to Madeline and started to explain.

"Well, it was your grandmother that changed my life."

He settled in, and Bailey knew she was in for a long story, but before he could get started, he was interrupted.

"Ah, excuse me while I take care of this matter," he said. "When I come back, I'll take you on a tour of the kitchen," he said, and was gone.

"Something's not adding up, here," Bailey said after he left.

"It's obvious that the whole layout of the shop, the items on the menu, even the decorations came from you. But he doesn't seem to know that."

"I told you, Evan is a rather mousy type of guy," Madeline offered.

"I'm pretty sure that Emma was leading him around by the nose. She probably had him thinking that everything was all her idea."

Evan returned quickly and ushered the two women out of their seats and into the back room. Even as busy as the shop was, he took the time to give them a brief tour of the kitchen, showing Madeline all of her ideas in full force. When the tour was finished, he was beaming from ear to ear.

Bailey took note of everything but was very confused. She decided she needed to go a little deeper than a casual observer.

"Evan," she started as they headed back toward the front of the store. "Where did you get your recipes that seem so popular today?"

"Well, to be honest," he said, "many of them came from my two business partners."

"Two business partners?" Madeline asked. She had only known about one, Emma.

"Yes," he continued. "Emma, you knew her,"—a look of sadness flitted across his face—"and my sister, Rachel."

"Oh, yes." Madeline remembered Rachel. The woman left a sour taste in her mouth. From what she recalled, Rachel was rather competitive and definitely was not inclined to the team effort that Evan, Emma, and Madeline had once had a long time ago.

"Well, she's here now!"

He said, and then turned in his seat to see if he could spot her in the crowd. He turned back.

"She must be in the back."

He paused for a moment before he continued. "It was so sad to hear about what happened to Emma." He waited for a response, but neither Madeline nor Bailey said anything.

"I didn't even know you two were still talking. I'd heard you had a major falling out a few years ago."

It was Madeline's turn to speak. "To be honest, Evan, I hadn't seen Emma in two years. I was just as surprised as you were that she had been in my store."

"I'm not surprised," Evan said thoughtfully. "She could be quite a pill when she wanted to."

"That she was," Madeline agreed.

"I don't know if you were aware of it," Evan continued, "but Emma and I had a major falling out of our own, just a few months ago."

Both Bailey and Madeline were trying to keep the confusion off their faces.

"We had to part ways," he continued. "Which was very sad since most of the décor, the recipes, and even the way we run things were her idea."

So, there it was. It appeared that Emma had only worked for Madeline in order to get at her secrets, and it seemed as if Evan was genuinely duped into doing whatever she said. Or he was a really good actor.

"So," Bailey interrupted. "What made you get into baking, Evan?"

Evan gave her a warm smile, and his face lit up as he reminisced about his past. You could tell he felt good about what he was remembering.

"I suppose it all started when I was small."

He settled in for what seemed like another long story. "I never knew my real parents," he said rather sadly. Don't really know what happened to them. No one was ever able to tell me. I was raised by a stream of foster parents from a young age."

It didn't seem like a happy story from the way he began, Bailey thought, but she wanted to know who this Evan guy really was. So she listened to his story without interrupting.

"It wasn't until I was about nine or ten that I landed in this home where my foster mom loved to bake."

His mouth curled up just a little at the corners as he thought about the woman. "She used to let me bake with her. It turned out it was the only thing that kept me stable. You can understand, I was quite an angry kid growing up. It felt like nobody really wanted me until I was sent to live with her."

He smiled even more. "It was her baking that gave my life some direction." He fell silent for a moment, lost in his own memories.

Bailey brought him back to the present. "Wow, that's interesting. But you said that my gran changed your life," she said. "How's that?"

"Oh!" Evan responded. He turned and gave Madeline an affectionate look.

"It was the competition," he said.

Emily Page

"I remember those meetings we used to have in preparation for the competition. Up until then, I only thought of baking as a kind of therapy, but you...you helped me see it as a business. From then on, I started seeing my baking skills in an entirely different way," he explained.

Bailey wanted to ask him more, but just then a young woman entered the store from the back room. Evan noticed her and beckoned for her to come over.

"There she is," he said. "I want you to meet my sister, Rachel."

Rachel approached the table the three of them were sitting at and gave her greetings.

"Good afternoon," she commented.

"Good afternoon, Rachel,"

Madeline said and offered her hand. Bailey noticed that her voice sounded tiny. She wondered why, but it wouldn't take too long for her to understand. Madeline knew Rachel all too well.

After introductions were made all around, Rachel joined in the conversation.

"Madeline," she started, "didn't you go to school with my brother?"

"Yes."

"And, don't you own The Baker's Shoppe over on Maple Street?"

"Yes," Madeline confirmed.

"Oh, yes," Rachel started.

"I'd love to ask you some questions," she said, almost as excited as Evan had been when he first saw Madeline.

"May I join you?"

She slid into the seat next to Madeline, eager to join the conversation. The four of them chatted away endlessly until well into the afternoon. Rachel plied Madeline with an endless array of questions about how she got into baking and where she came up with her ideas for her store. She also offered her condolences for Emma's death.

"How is it that the three of you became such good friends?" she asked.

"Well, it's like any other classmates you have when you're in school," Madeline offered.

"You just have some classmates that you click with."

"I suppose," Rachel agreed.

"I guess I never had anyone that I 'clicked' with," she said, making the quotation marks with her fingers. She glanced over at her brother.

"I guess it's Evan who has that friendship gene, not me."

"I'm impressed," Bailey commented. "Do you have the same feelings as Evan about your foster mom?"

Rachel fell silent for a moment while she remembered her childhood years. "I knew her," she finally answered, "but I didn't have the same relationship with her as Evan did."

"Really?" Bailey thought, out loud.

"Well, I was pretty much a loner when I came to live in the house."

"Oh, you didn't come together?"

Both Evan and Rachel laughed. "No. We're not really brother and sister," Evan explained.

"We're both just foster kids who spent part of their childhood in the same house."

"Oh," Madeline interjected. "I never knew that. I thought you were really brother and sister."

"No. A lot of people think that," Evan added.

"So, Madeline," Rachel interrupted.

"Tell me, where did you get the inspiration for your ideas about the store?"

The conversation went on with questions flowing back and forth until the store became too busy and both Evan and Rachel had to say their good-byes and get back to work.

CHAPTER NINE

Madeline returned to her store, and for the next few days things seemed almost as if nothing had changed. Life slowly began to return to normal for her as she went about her daily activities. Still, nothing changed in regard to finding Emma's murderer, and the case weighed heavily on her mind.

So, she wasn't too surprised when, at the height of the business rush, she saw Nolan enter her store and take up his usual position at a corner table, where he could observe all the comings and goings of her business. She knew he was looking for something but so far had been unable to find it.

Nolan said nothing when he came in, but waited patiently for the rush of the early morning patrons to thin out. He made the girls nervous whenever he came in, and they had a hard time concentrating on their work, but Madeline seemed much less threatened by his presence now that she had been doing her own investigating. Emma, it turned out, didn't have too many friends, and those that she did have were soon to become victims of her conniving plots and schemes; it was just a matter of time.

When everything had quieted down, Madeline poured a cup of coffee, took it over to Nolan, and slid into the chair across from him while the girls went about the cleaning up and restocking that always came after a good morning rush.

"Morning, Chief,"

Madeline said with as friendly a greeting as she could.

Nolan set down the paper he was reading and gave her his full attention. "Morning."

"Can I get you anything?" Madeline offered, her voice lacking any form of sincerity.

"Sure," Nolan said. "How about a cup of coffee?"

Madeline shoved the cup she had brought over in front of him.

Nolan looked at the cup and then at Madeline. The inquisitive arch of one eyebrow questioned her.

"You see, Chief," she said,

"I used my own deductive reasoning and determined that you wanted a cup of coffee."

"Oh really. How's that?" Nolan asked. He decided to appease her and follow along for the moment.

"Well," Madeline started,

"I noticed that every now and then you come into my store, take up a table all by yourself, and you never order anything." She was very calm and composed as she spoke.

"But, I figured he wouldn't just be coming in here at the busiest time of the day, taking away space from my customers, just to harass me. He must want something."

She let her voice slow down just a little bit. "After all, I can't imagine any officer of the law interfering with the flow of business that way." She proffered him a soft smile.

"So, you must be here for my famous coffee and at least one of my tasty treats."

Nolan looked at the woman across the table from him. She was pretty smart, there was no doubt about it. But he still felt strongly that she had something to do with Emma's murder. He'd bet his forty-year career on it.

"Ok, Mrs. McDougal. I'll bite," he said.

"Why don't you give me one of those praline pastries that everyone seemed so gung ho about."

"Sure thing, Chief." Madeline got up from her seat and collected the pastry he had requested.

When she returned, Nolan was waiting for her. She slid into the seat opposite him and quietly waited until he had sweetened his coffee and taken a bite of her praline. A satisfying smile crossed his lips before he spoke.

"I see why your business has become so popular. These are amazing," he said with sincerity.

Madeline thought that she was witnessing the first sign of a human being in Nolan since they had first met. "Thank you."

"But," Nolan said as he took another bite,

"I have to remind you that you're still a person of interest on the case." He sipped his cup of coffee and turned his attention back to Madeline.

"Don't even think about taking a vacation or anything like that."

"Of course," Madeline said with unusual calm.

Nolan looked at her with genuine surprise. She was not reacting as she had done before, and he was not prepared for the sublime acceptance of his accusation. Madeline, on the other hand, had become accustomed to the man's empty threats. It was clear that he would never have the evidence to actually charge her with anything. In the meantime, she, Bailey, and Kyle were making headway on their own investigation. They had not yet offered anything to the police, but they certainly had accumulated enough to put Nolan and his hound dogs on a different scent if it ever came to that.

Nolan finished his last bite of the praline, all too soon, he thought. It was no wonder her bakery had become so popular over the years. He'd never had a breakfast treat like that.

"Awesome pastry," he said as he tossed a five dollar bill on the table.

"I hope that'll be enough to cover it."

He lifted his mighty bulk up from his seat, gave her a curt farewell, and then started for the door.

Nolan had left pretty much the way he usually came. In a big huff. A lot of wind but no substance, Madeline thought to herself. Still, there was that nagging doubt in the back of her mind that she had to do something to get him off her scent. Even an old dog would find a bone if he rooted around long enough. She knew Nolan was looking for just one crumb of substantial evidence he could manipulate in order to implicate her, so she had to step up her efforts to beat him at his own game. It was time for her, Bailey, and Kyle to have another meeting.

The store closed early for a change. Madeline, Bailey, and Kyle were meeting in the back room, trying to determine what made Nolan so determined to focus all of his attention on Madeline. Kyle was pacing back and forth across the small room while Bailey was busily typing away at the keyboard of her laptop. She had gathered all the evidence they had found so far in one place so she didn't have to carry around her cumbersome notebook. It was stored on her flash drive, which she could conveniently stash away when she needed to. Madeline was sitting behind the desk deep in thought.

"He doesn't have anything on you,"

Kyle said as he stopped his pacing to face her. "I don't think you have anything to worry about. Everything he has is circumstantial."

"Yeah, but that's the problem," Bailey said.

"If he keeps digging, he'll come up with something that might stick. All he needs is something that a jury will believe."

"True, but what does he have?"

"You keep talking about what he has," Bailey complained. "It's not what he has that concerns us. It's what he might find."

"Ok. Ok," Kyle said. "What could he possibly find on Madeline?" he asked, trying to appease her.

"All right, let's see." She got up from her seat and started pacing opposite Kyle. "She was the one to find the body."

"Yeah, but that could've been anybody," Kyle argued.

"It was at her place of business."

"But it was outside the business, not inside."

"They had been rivals for years."

"They hadn't seen each other in years, so why kill her now?" Kyle countered.

"Witnesses saw them in a heated argument."

"Two years ago."

The two were simply at odds on Madeline's true position in the eyes of the police.

"Ok. Let me tell you why you shouldn't be concerned," Kyle said.

"First, she has no history of anger problems, ever. Second, she has a strong relationship with the community with impeccable character."

He finished his last statement with a sense of finality that said that his last words should've been enough to determine her innocence all on their own.

"I'm telling you that Nolan's argument doesn't have a leg to stand on."

"Well, she's still a suspect, no matter what you think, believe, or know," she said with exasperation. "We have to do something."

"Well Nolan has to have more to arouse his suspicions than we know, otherwise he wouldn't be so persistent," Madeline finally spoke up.

"I know why he's so persistent," Bailey countered. "Because she's being set up."

"No. I have a better reason," Kyle countered. "He's an incompetent boob."

CHAPTER TEN

The three sat and discussed the case well into the evening. It seemed that they had reached an impasse. Nothing was moving forward. Not only were they unable to come up with a few reasons that could convince Nolan Madeline wasn't a viable suspect, but they also were unable to provide an alternative suspect. As long as Nolan was unwilling to look at anyone else, it was evident that Madeline would be persona non grata in his eyes.

"I know what we have to do," Bailey announced.

Madeline looked at her granddaughter and recognized that firm determination in her eyes.

"We have to root out the killer."

"What do you mean?"

"We need to do something to force his hand, force him to expose himself."

"That's a mighty big plan, Bailey," Kyle said. "Considering we don't know who the killer is."

"Well, we have some pretty good ideas," Bailey countered. "I'm pretty sure that one of these people on our list is the killer"

She waved her hand at her opened computer screen.

"All we need to do is to get them to think we suspect them. They'll be forced to do something to cover their tracks."

Kyle stared at Bailey and Madeline for a long while. He was worried that the women were getting in over their heads. This was not some petty crime they were trying to solve. They were trying to find someone who would stop at nothing to get what they wanted.

"Maybe we should hold back a bit," he said, trying to subtly backpedal to distract them from the case.

"Hold back?" Madeline said.

"Not when my head is on the chopping block." She turned her full gaze on Kyle.

"Listen, I know that you're concerned about what could happen, but frankly, I'm getting tired of my little trysts with Nolan," she said with no little frustration.

"I want this whole affair to be over before it ruins my business."

"I understand," Kyle said, trying to assuage her. "But I just think it's too risky at this point."

"What do you suggest?" Bailey asked.

"I think we should take everything we've put together and pass it on to a private detective," he suggested. "Let them take it from here."

Madeline thought that Kyle had a point, but she wasn't willing to put her trust in another stranger. She wanted to keep her hand in the mix.

"Let's try one more thing before we do that," she suggested.

"What's that?" Kyle asked.

"Well, let's see. Who do we suspect so far?"

Bailey referred to her copious notes. "Well, we have Evan Foster. He's obviously the one that Emma had been feeding your secrets to. Then we have Kelsey Bryson, the mayor's wife.

And of course, we also have a list of men who've been reported to have slept with her and then been blackmailed into giving her financial support."

"All right," Madeline said, stopping her. "Let's start with the most likely suspect. The one we have the most evidence on."

"That would be Evan Foster."

"But from what you ladies told me, he didn't seem like a potential suspect when you went to visit him.

"Yeah, but he admitted that he and Emma had had a recent falling out."

"I admit that the theory has legs, but we need more proof. That's the same argument Nolan has against you."

Madeline got up from her chair, engrossed in thought.

"Why don't we sweeten the pot just a bit?" she said.

"Dangle a carrot in front of him and see if he'll take the bait."

"I don't know," Kyle began to protest. "It's sounds too risky."

"Listen, when you see Evan, you'll see how much of a pussycat he really is," Madeline assured him.

"Let's just try this one thing, and if it doesn't pan out, we'll call an investigator."

She made an X across her chest with her index finger and then held up her right hand with the palm facing Kyle.

"Cross my heart."

She gave him an innocent smile. "Besides, what's he gonna do if all three of us are there?"

Kyle reluctantly agreed to the plan, and the three of them put their heads together to try to develop a strategy that would force Evan's hand.

The three of them entered Evan's shop and took a spot in a corner booth, where they could have a good vantage point to see the rest of the store. Evan was behind the counter, but he gave them a friendly wave when they entered, clearly elated to see them again. The store was not as busy today as it was the other day, which was the way Madeline had planned it. She didn't want a lot of people around just in case things went wrong.

Evan approached the table as soon as he got a minute free. He turned the register over to Rachel and came and joined the trio.

"Wow," he said. "I never thought I'd see you again so soon."

"Well, Evan," Madeline started,

"I must confess, this is not at all a social call. In fact, I have a little business proposition for you."

Evan's eyes narrowed into an inquisitive slant. "With you?" he asked. "I'm intrigued."

"Well, not here," Madeline said. "Can you stop by my store, tomorrow after closing?"

She could tell that Evan's curiosity was peaked.

"Of course," he said.

"But I'm afraid we stay open kind of late these days." He thought for a minute.

"Maybe I could leave Rachel in charge for a while."

"Well, we close at around five every day. How about you come by at around five thirty, six?"

Evan gave her a wide grin. "It's a date."

He handed the trio a bag of treats before they left. It was apparent that he was quite ecstatic at the prospect of a business relationship with Madeline.

Evan proved to be extremely punctual, arriving at the store at precisely five thirty. He was clearly eager to find out what Madeline had to say. She ushered him into her back office, where Bailey was already waiting. Bailey gave him a friendly greeting and gestured for him to take a seat across from Madeline's desk.

"I have to admit, Madeline," Evan started, "that I could hardly sleep last night thinking of the possibility of joining forces with you on a new business venture."

"Well, Evan, my proposition is not anything as grand as that.

"Oh really?" He looked a little disappointed. "Then what is it?"

Bailey rose from her seat and walked over to Evan and tossed the little red notebook onto the desk in front of him. "It's this," she said.

Evan's face clouded over as he looked at the book. Confused, he stared at it as though he wasn't sure if it would bite him or not.

"What is it?" he asked.

"Why don't you tell us?" Bailey said, her tone switching from slippery sweet to cutting.

Surprised, Evan gingerly picked up the book and turned it over in his hands. "I don't know what it is."

"Open it," Madeline said. "Look inside."

He opened it, and the surprise that ran across his face was genuine. After only a few seconds of flipping through the pages, he said,

"These are all the ideas that Emma gave me for my store."

"Correction," Madeline countered. "Those are all the ideas that Emma stole from me and gave to you for your store."

Evan's mouth flew open. He was appalled at the accusation. "What are you trying to say?" he questioned, obviously hurt.

"Well, Evan, I'd like you to take a walk around my store and tell me if you see anything familiar about it."

"Why would you want me to do that?" he asked.

Madeline rose from her seat. "I insist," she said. "My attorney, Kyle, will escort you."

Kyle appeared in the doorway precisely on cue, standing erect and buttoning up his jacket with an air of sophistication.

"Go on," Madeline said. She waved her hands in front of him as if to send away a small child. "Shoo. Shoo. I'll be here when you get back."

Evan thought about refusing, but one look at Kyle standing there looking like the mafia made him think twice. He rose and followed Kyle around the store.

A few minutes later, the two men returned, and Evan's face was distraught. "I don't understand," he commented.

"My store has been here for more than ten years now, and as you can see, Evan, all the ideas you got from Emma were stolen from me."

"What are you saying?" he asked. "Are you implying that Emma and I had some arrangement to steal your business?"

"That's exactly what I'm implying," Madeline continued.

"But something happened between you two and she threatened to expose you as a fraud."

"What?"

"So, you lured her over here, set a trap, and killed her in my store so that I would get framed for it."

Evan's face evolved from shock to horror. He was appalled that the woman he had such high esteem for would believe such a thing. He spread his hands out in front of him as if to plead for her to understand.

"Madeline," he said, "you know me. We've been friends for so long. How could you think this of me?"

"Evan, it is obvious from this book that Emma was stealing from me and feeding you my ideas. Are you saying that you knew nothing about it?"

"Yes, that's what I'm saying," he said defiantly. His voice was beginning to tremble a little.

"I didn't know she was stealing from you. I swear!" he said with a little more trembling and a sniffle to add to it.

Madeline and Bailey sat horrified as they watched the man crumble right before their eyes. They were shocked when they saw a tear start to form, and they began to have second thoughts about their accusation.

"Maddie," he said, "you know I've always admired and respected you. How could you think of me in this way? I'm just a poor kid that grew up in a string of foster homes. I know what it's like to build something from scratch and to make something out of nothing like you did. If it wasn't for my Mama Betty and you, then my successes would all have likely been failures. She was the only one who took the time to teach me how to be a decent human being. I swore I would never do anything that would disappoint her in any way." He stopped speaking to sniffle a little bit more.

"You always reminded me of her, Maddie. That's why I always looked up to you."

Madeline and Bailey both looked on, speechless. They weren't sure if they were watching a well-rehearsed performance or were observing the real man.

Evan continued. "I often shared my fondest memories of our times together at culinary school. I always told Rachel about them and the fun times we had."

He smiled a little, more to himself than those who were looking on. Kyle rolled his eyes and decided to excuse himself from seeing any more.

"I'm sorry, Evan," Madeline said. "I was clearly mistaken, and I apologize profusely."

Bailey looked at her grandmother in stunned silence.

"I'm so sorry to have to put you through this, Evan, but we had to be sure," Madeline assured him. "I hope we can continue to be friends after this."

Evan didn't answer right away. He had drifted off into deep thought. Finally he spoke.

"It was always pretty hard for us growing up, Rachel and me. But if it wasn't for Mama Betty, chances are we'd have had very different lives."

Madeline wondered why he was telling them this.

"Did you ever wonder how it was that I got into culinary school?" He smiled to himself.

"I won a cooking scholarship. Both Rachel and I entered, but there could only be one winner. She got second place and I won first."

He smiled a little bit. "We were so proud that our family had swept the competition. When I went to school, I always came home and taught her everything I had learned."

Evan continued to reminisce for a while as Madeline and Bailey watched. They were convinced now that they had pegged the wrong person as the killer. Evan didn't have a murderous bone in his body. Bailey looked around and wanted to kill Kyle for sneaking off the way he did, and she chided herself for not thinking of it first.

She slowly inched her way to the doorway and was standing there trying to figure out how to get out of the sad story when the door flung open and an arm flung violently around her neck. She only needed to see the glint of the knife and feel the sharp edge of its point against her throat to know that their plan had actually worked and they had flushed out the killer.

Madeline and Evan leaped from their seats, startled by the noise, and turned to see Rachel, her eyes fierce like a wild animal's, standing there with a knife to Bailey's throat. Madeline screamed, but she dared not move in Bailey's direction. Evan looked at his sister in horror.

"Rachel!" he shouted. "What're you doing?"

"You stupid idiot," she shouted at Evan.

"Why don't you just stop talking all the time? You've gone and destroyed everything," she complained.

Bailey tried to pull away while Rachel was focused on Evan, but Rachel was surprisingly strong.

"Yes. I killed Emma and I did it so that I could get rid of all you silly sentimentalists," she shouted.

"Rachel," Evan pleaded. "You don't want to do this," he said soothingly.

"Shut up! You blithering idiot!" she spat.

"Of course I want to do this, if only to get rid of you and your weak little attitude." She started backing toward the door, pulling Bailey with her.

"All you ever did was talk about how nice Mrs. Madeline was, how great Mama Betty was to you, and how much you admired and respected them. You never had a thought of your own in your entire life."

Evan looked shocked and hurt by her accusations.

"And so what happens? The one with absolutely no originality, no ideas, no sense of creativity gets a scholarship and gets to go to culinary school while I, who had been with Mama Betty far longer than you, got to sit at home and babysit. It was so unfair."

Evan tried once again. "Rachel, why didn't you talk to me about this before?"

"Because you had too many stars in your eyes for Madeline and Mama Betty. You wouldn't have seen what I saw: two selfish women who had nothing to give anyone who didn't kowtow to their every wish," she answered.

"But you know what the worst part of it was?" she asked. "What hurt the most?" she waited for a response.

"When you decided to open up your own bakery, you turned to vindictive Emma and her unscrupulous tactics instead of your own sister. The one who had helped you your entire life."

"I didn't know you wanted to be in the business," Evan said defensively.

"You should've asked," she shouted at him. "Imagine what the two of us together could have accomplished," she said dreamily, tears now streaming down her face.

"And when you finally hired me to work behind your counter, I was hurt, really hurt." Her eyes now spilled tears that made little lines down her face.

"You chose Emma, the little slut, the little thief, the liar, for a partner instead of me?" She backed a few more steps toward the door.

"Yes," she said.

"Yes, I killed Emma, and I planted that little book in here too. I figured if I killed Emma and the book was here, they would blame Evan for the murder. With you in jail, little brother, I could take over the business and get what I always deserved."

As she pulled Bailey through the door, she relaxed her grip just enough. Thinking that she had gotten clear of the danger, she had thought to take Bailey someplace remote and get rid of her, but as she rounded the corner with her hostage, a strong arm came out of nowhere and twisted her knife-wielding arm behind her back, forcing her to release her grip on Bailey. She screamed from the pain, and through tear-filled eyes, she saw Kyle's large frame towering over her.

Bailey, realizing she was free, ran across the room to where Madeline was reaching out to catch her, as she always did.

Kyle took Rachel and forcibly pushed her down in a chair while Madeline called the police. From the other side of the room, she could feel Evan watching her closely, his eyes red and his face stained from his own tears.

He got up and slowly approached Rachel, pulling up a chair and turning it to face her.

"Why, Rachel?" he asked. "Why would you do such a horrific thing?"

"Shut up!" she snapped. "Shut up and be a man for a change."

"Rachel," he said.

"All you had to do was ask me. You know I would've given you anything you wanted. And now an innocent woman is dead."

"Innocent?" Rachel laughed.

"You were so much in love with Emma that you didn't see her for what she really was." She gave a derisive laugh.

"Emma was far from innocent. And I knew all along that you suspected Evan," she said to Madeline.

"Well I didn't really suspect him right away," Madeline countered.

"Of course you did," Rachel corrected.

"You suspected him two years ago, when you fired Emma for stealing your secrets. You never thought it was me, because none of you ever gave me a second thought. So, when Emma approached me about helping Evan get out of catering and enter his own business, no one thought about me. I knew that Emma had her own ideas, but it was your ideas that were selling. She told me that she had a master key to your shop and she could get in any time, day or night. I knew she could help play into my plan."

"I had her call me several times a week and tell me exactly what you were doing, and then we implemented the same thing in our business, just with a little more finesse. Things were going real good for a while, but then Emma got greedy. She wanted more money, and Evan was just the sniveling idiot to give it to her. If they had continued to run the business, chances are we would've eventually had to close. We couldn't keep supporting Emma's habits. She was running through money like water through a sieve. As much as we were making, we were losing."

She called me one night and asked me to meet her here after your business closed. She wanted to show me something, but she didn't say what it was. I watched you leave that night, Mrs. Madeline. I watched you lock up your store and walk home with that stupid looking cat. Then Emma came and let me in the back door. She said she wanted to talk, but she really wanted to kill me. She felt I had too much influence over Evan, and he wanted to stop giving her money. I thought she was speaking crazy talk, so I walked out.

"That's when she pulled out her gun and tried to kill me. But I grew up on the streets, I know how to fight and I managed to get the gun away from her." Rachel laughed in derision.

"I realized that nothing would be the same again, so I turned the tables on her. I shot her. I shot her right there in the back alley."

"I knew that the police would blame Madeline for the murder, Madeline would blame Evan, and no one would suspect me. Not little old me, who had never done anything of significance in her whole life."

Rachel laughed a wicked little laugh. "Not little Rachel," she said to herself and then she fell completely quiet.

For the second time in as many weeks, Madeline's storefront was filled with police officers. Rachel sat in a chair with her hands cuffed behind her back. Nolan stood by as he watched deputies pull Rachel from the chair and lead her out the door.

"Well, I have to admit, Mrs. McDougal, I had you pegged all wrong."

He picked up a muffin off the counter and looked at her straight.

"I suppose we should all have a little celebration or something. You know, in honor of catching a real killer. Maybe you could provide the cupcakes."

Madeline looked at Nolan as if he had just landed from another planet.

Nolan took the look as an opportunity to try to bury the hatchet.

"Oh, if I remember correctly, you wanted me to call you Maddie, right? Instead of Mrs. McDougal?"

Maddie thought for a moment. "No, Chief. I believe you were right the first time. Call me Mrs. McDougal."

A Special Delivery To Die For:

In an effort to expand her business, bakery owner Madeline McDougal debuts a new Home Delivery service. One of her first stops is the home of local business owner and travel agent Ana Stevens. Upon her arrival however Madeline to her surprise finds the front door of Ana's house open... and later to her shock and horror, she discovers Ana's dead body lying on the floor inside!

Determined to find Ana's killer, Madeline and her friends begin to sift through a quartet of suspects. Will the killer catch on and make them their next target?

Find out what Maddie discovers in book two of The Rockcrest Cove Mysteries! Get Your Copy Today!

www.ingramcontent.com/pod-product-compliance
Lightning Source LLC
Chambersburg PA
CBHW070852120626
46556CB00002B/960